The Forest Museum

ISBN (paperback): 978-1-959153-00-9
ISBN (ebook): 978-1-959153-01-6

ALBATROSS BOOK CO.
www.albatrossbookco.com

The Forest Museum

Written & Illustrated
by Pip Craighead

1.

In the summer of 1972, Celeste Nascimento — a young painter fresh out of an American art school — was hired to retouch the 18th-century landscape paintings which hung within the hall of a hunting lodge upon a grand estate in Germany's Black Forest. The estate, the Schloss Fernweh, was once the wilderness retreat of a wealthy Bavarian family with vague, unenumerated ties to royalty. Every day of her stay Celeste was to dutifully work away at restoring the paintings, which depicted dark-eyed stags and bright-eyed rabbits running over vast, rolling hills of finely manicured grass, with walls of geometrically spaced trees looming in the distance.

Two centuries ago, those pictures were painted straight onto the upper half of the walls, and so it was that Celeste found herself often working in physically straining positions, standing on a ladder at odd angles in order to reach particular details. As a result, she could only put in two to three hours of work each day before her neck or arms started to ache fiercely, at which point she would put her tools away and spend the rest of the afternoon exploring the sprawling environs of the country estate.

Celeste had grown up in Patagonia, Arizona, a small town just north of the Mexican border, and as a teenager living in the glare of an unrelenting sun, she had often dreamt of the cool eaves of far-off European forests. Many afternoons she'd hid herself within the air-conditioned microcosm of the town library, gazing wistfully at Time-Life compendiums of Renaissance art and medieval castles, imagining what it would be like to explore those immense tracts of ancient woodland. "Europe," she would think to herself, "people used to just call it *The Continent.*" In her mind, she saw fathomless swathes of untrammeled grass sprawling out in sloping curves, and in the distance, ice-capped mountains that reared up into the sky, great shards of sheer-sided stone thrust up from the earth's inscrutable interior. She envisioned crystalline sunbeams falling upon marble manors, and long corridors of trees forming lush green bowers of leaves that stretched off into the horizon, flanked by colonnades of pale white trunks, and when the wind rose, the leaves would catch the light and throw off shimmering flashes of silver.

So it was with a great sense of relish that Celeste was now here, in the land she'd dreamt of, having graduated from California's Chouinard Art Institute and found summer work restoring these antiquarian paintings. She did not necessarily feel a sense of connection with the actual Europeans she met; to the contrary, European society made her feel more distinctly aware of her Americanness, in a strange inversion of the way she had felt like a displaced European when among certain Americans in her hometown. But whatever alienation she felt in her encounters with European society, she felt profoundly connected to the European landscape. Somehow nature here felt precisely curated to her, as if every part had been arranged just so, even down to the manner in which fallen branches lay akimbo upon the wet green earth after a storm. It was as if the whole world were the grounds of a vast, nameless estate, or a boundless garden. There was a stillness in the air out here, like that of an enormous outdoor museum.

2.

One day, as Celeste strolled the undulating lawns and shadowy groves of the forested estate in the light of the late afternoon, she found her mind drifting to a single-screen theater in the Arizonan suburbs where she'd first seen *The Sound of Music,* in the summer of 1966. Specifically, she recalled sitting in a plush red seat within the darkened cinema, watching the scenes which took place inside a glass gazebo upon the lush grounds of the Von Trapp estate.

Those scenes, while containing some footage shot in Salzburg, were filmed primarily on the 20th Century Fox studio lot in Los Angeles, where within the cavernous confines of a Culver City soundstage, set decorators had fashioned a recreation of an Austrian night scene: a shadowy orchard of moonlit mists creeping upon a lush green lawn, the gazebo structure glowing white against the deep blue of the evening — an artificial European nocturne staged upon the far edge of the New World, a few miles from where the Pacific lapped upon the western rim of North America.

Celeste recalled reading somewhere that one of the Fox studio executives had lived in Austria as a child and, while visiting the *Sound of Music* set as it was being filmed in August 1964, found that this simulated scene touched something deep within him. So one night, when everyone but the guards had gone home, this executive surreptitiously made his way to the soundstage, carrying with him a sleeping bag and pillow. After asking a night guard to make sure he was undisturbed, the executive made his bed upon the artificial grass and fell asleep beneath the perpetual glow of the artificial moon, a smile upon his face.

That executive knew something of the strange feeling which Celeste now sensed while walking the grounds of the Fernweh estate. She felt as if she had somehow entered into that feeling of endlessness which the Technicolor matte paintings of certain Hollywood films often evoked in her, the feeling of an unchanging background filled with promise, an aesthetic impulse which seemed to her to link up to the tradition of landscape painting from medieval times to now.

3.

Every afternoon, Celeste would wander the seemingly endless realm of the estate, which was bounded by a high green hedge upon its southern, eastern, and western edges. She had been told by one of the groundskeepers that the northern border lay within the crepuscular interior of the forest, demarcated at a certain point by an ancient fence of ragged wooden slats, whose worth as a border lay in its symbolic value rather than serving as any practical impediment to trespassers. Celeste, however, had not yet gone far enough into the dim world of the forest to encounter the fence herself.

Walking around the woodland world — which felt to her somehow like a miniature terrarium, a microcosm sealed within a bottle — Celeste assembled an interior library of images and feelings, small scenes which she filed away in the innumerable cabinets of her mind:

The glowing of damask rose petals as they lay silently upon the wet black earth. The narcotic motion of the wind across fields of tall standing grass, its invisible passage made visible in the rippling movements of grass blades as it ran along them, ruffling their hair and making them dance. The way of an eagle in the sky, cresting high above the earth, pinions shining dully in the sun. Reeds silently undulating beneath the translucent surface of a river, their pale green tendrils swaying languidly as currents gently passed through the hermetic land of aquatic vegetation and murky silt floors which carpeted the modest corridors of the river, beside moss-robed stones smoothed by long centuries. The sharply evocative sensation which came over Celeste when, toward the end of the day, she could see a procession of farmers on their journey home, trudging through a shadowy forest lane with their wooden carts and laden horses, even as the late afternoon sun cast the outer eaves of the woods in flowing hues of gold.

At night, when she sat in the immeasurably comfortable golden-satin armchairs of the great hall, staring at the flickering terpsichorean motions of the fire, Celeste would roll over the collection of these moments in her mind. What was the sum of them? Individually, they were by turns comforting and charming, picturesque or strangely haunting, pierced with a kind of pleasing loneliness or quiet stillness. But when she surveyed them all together, lined up like dioramas on display in a museum, they felt like they *meant* something, something whose importance could not be overstated; they felt cosmically potent. When experienced individually, they were pleasing and light; taken as a whole, they felt immeasurably heavy, as if burdened with the secrets of the universe, pregnant with a message of life-or-death importance.

Celeste's evening ruminations would grow ever more abstract with encroaching drowsiness, and would gradually dissolve into incoherence as she was overcome by sleep, her consciousness unhitching from its mooring and slowly drifting into the golden haze of slumber's open ocean. Into the mirrored hallways of memory she would go, past chambers of her mind filled with subterranean treasures, past luminous minerals darkly sparkling amid lugubrious caves, and through doorways which led variously to moon-misted swamps, and Antarctic ice floes where half-sunk galleons lay rimed with hoarfrost, and endless rolling hills were illumined by sullen dawns.

4.

Nine mornings into her stay upon the grand estate, Celeste found herself gazing out the window of the second-story bathroom, brushing her teeth after an early breakfast. Crisp rays of early sunlight fell through the oriel window upon mauve tiles patterned with arabesque designs. Standing there, she thought of what lay beyond that window: the unseen entirety of Europe at dawn — a vast continent swathed in shafts of roseate light, which streamed down through breaks in the clouds as they rolled along and collided in slow motion, incorporeal glaciers of diffused precipitation.

Celeste decided that today, after putting in her time restoring the paintings, she would go into the forest and find the fence which marked the estate's northern border. According to a map of the property which was on display in the dining hall, the fence did not appear to lie especially deep in the woods; the boundary appeared to be less than a mile into the forest. With that thought, Celeste bounded down the stairs, cheerful with the sense of a new day and a goal for her afternoon. As she passed out the door of the servants' quarters in which she was staying, she saw a member of the domestic staff and said hello. The woman in question, who was carrying a wicker basket filled with freshly laundered white linens, gave a perfunctory nod. The staff who Celeste had encountered here were few — the entire estate seemed to be run by scarcely a dozen people — and while not unfriendly, they remained quiet and somewhat inscrutable. Celeste found it hard to tell what they thought of her, and wondered if this was the result of unbroken centuries of a tradition of servitude or was merely her American perception of a certain European coolness.

Celeste's three hours of painting that morning were spent entirely focused on the gray hindquarters of a hunting dog that was pictured mid-stride, bounding along a rounded green hill in pursuit of a formidable stag that stood, glancing back at its pursuers, in the far-right horizon of the painting.

When Celeste had first arrived at the estate, she'd unpacked a small aquamarine-plastic transistor radio she'd brought with her to accompany the hours of painting. But she found that when she actually tried playing it, the German and American pop tunes which filled the room felt tinny and hollow, and profoundly inappropriate, breaking the pregnant silence of the room as if shattering the icy surface of a half-frozen lake. Even the classical station felt oddly disruptive. She contented herself with painting in quiet now, and as always happens when one is doing something in silence, the background ambience of the room and surrounding environs seemed to amplify, foregrounding the incidental creaking of wood, the cheerful songs of rock-thrushes and scrub-robins outside, and the rhythmic click of distant gardening shears. Celeste found, rather counter-intuitively, that the more she paid attention to this hushed soundtrack, the more interesting she found it, and instead of being a random assortment of haphazard sounds, it began in her mind to resemble more and more a carefully assembled tapestry, almost a musical composition of sorts. She felt she had discovered a symphony of inestimable length which was ever unfolding, playing at such a low volume that it became a stealth music, a song everyone on Earth is listening to but which nobody realizes they are hearing.

So it was that she spent three hours listening to this hidden music while painting. Once her neck and right arm began to ache, she decided to break for the day, climbing down the ladder and cleaning her tools. After a quick lunch, she made for the woods, and found she couldn't help but smile as she strode along the crisp green grass with sunshine falling all around her, turning wisps of her dark hair golden in the bright noonday air.

The edge of the forest itself began somewhat abruptly upon the northern lawn; the trees had been cleared in a straight line so that the delineation between meadowy estate grounds and wood-land was geometrically precise, as plainly cut and dry as the boundaries of a forest appear on a map. As Celeste stepped onto the winding dirt path that led into the forest, she was conscious of crossing a threshold of some sort, and within a few moments the very air she breathed seemed to change correspondingly: the breeze fell away and the atmosphere became damper and cooler, while the sunlight, though still cheerfully filtering through the canopy of the trees, grew dimmer. The fresh scent of the open meadow was replaced by more earthy smells: the fragrance of fertile soil, of moss and fungi growing on bark, of wet loam and wild mushrooms. Celeste felt as if she were stepping into an older era, into a tract of time left over from centuries prior.

The path before her was smooth and well-kept, though the hoary tendrils of twisted roots occa-sionally thrust themselves across the way. The trail initially skirted along the edge of the forest, heading westward, but then turned and went north into the heart of the woods. Venerable pines and spruces loomed darkly upon either side of the lane, inter-spersed with beeches and oaks. Beyond the edges of the path, fallen leaves carpeted the black soil. It did not feel like being outside, Celeste thought to herself; rather, it felt like being inside a great, airy room, or perhaps a warehouse. The sounds of warbler and blackbird seemed to echo off the trunks of trees, and beneath it all, there was an almost tangible sense of things continually growing, growing, growing as they had for many long years.

5.

Celeste walked lightly along, taking in the dark riches of the fragrant forest. Her awareness of the time passing and the distance traveled receded into the back of her mind, and for about an hour she headed deeper into the woodland in a state of happy oblivion. The path itself would occasionally turn and wind, sometimes in response to the lay of the land — to avoid, say, the imposing figure of a great, weathered tree trunk — and other times as if in accordance with its own unknowable whims, but it always eventually resumed its way northward.

One such bend in the trail took Celeste around a thicket of densely clustered firs, the interior of which was rife with undergrowth. The fir leaves within were still studded with morning dew, with trembling droplets like ovoid jewels clinging to the waxy emerald needles.

The path curved around, and then Celeste suddenly stopped in her tracks, for a few feet before her, a turkey-like bird stood in the middle of the way.

Celeste recognized it as a capercallie, or wood grouse, which she had read somewhere was the symbolic bird of the Black Forest (though who determines such things? she wondered as an aside). It was standing there in the hushed stillness of the woods, its plumage faintly glistening. Its feathers were mostly black, mottled with dabs of white, while its wings were a rich brown, and above the dark bead of each of its eyes there was a crest of scarlet, like an exaggerated arched eyebrow. Its chest was colored a bluish-green which seemed to glow faintly, while its beak was a wan yellow.

Staring mutely at the bird's plumage, Celeste realized that a considerable amount of time had passed since she had entered the wood. Having come this far north into the forest interior, she most certainly should have encountered the border fence by this point. Celeste looked round about her. An unbroken horizon of trees stretched far away in every direction, firs and spruces and oaks in endless succession. A few moths fluttered erratically in the air, their pale wings catching the sunlight falling through the living gauze of the forest roof. There was a great stillness here, as if the woodland were holding its breath in anticipation — anticipation of what, Celeste did not know. She took in the scene, and became aware that her own breathing had slowed as if in complementary deference to the placid *tableau vivant* before her.

The capercaillie grew restless and ambled off the path, disappearing into a patch of mantis-green foliage. Celeste decided to turn and head back to the mansion; perhaps there she would take another look at the map of the estate to see if she had misread the location of the northern fence. Her walk back was uneventful, and upon her return she promptly forgot about the map, deciding instead to spend the rest of the afternoon reading beside the reflecting pool, in the shade of a Greek-columned pavilion.

6.

Celeste was sitting in a poolside recliner and drowsily reading a battered Penguin paperback edition of Turgenev's *Sketches from a Hunter's Album*, while reflections from the water cast brightly undulating circles upon her face, when a voice, unexpectedly close, wakened her from her state of late afternoon torpor.

"So you're a painter?" said the voice, which was friendly and reedy, speaking in an English colored by a heavy Alemannic accent. Startled, Celeste turned to the speaker: a short, thin man with a mustache and somewhat shaggy dark-brown hair. He looked like he was in his thirties but had a certain affable boyishness about him, and was dressed in a ribbed green cardigan and corduroy pants which flared at the bottom. Seeing Celeste's look of surprise, he blushed slightly.

"I'm sorry, I didn't mean to startle you," he said earnestly, starting to back up as if to leave. "I will come back another time."

"No, no, it's quite all right," Celeste interjected. She felt a bit embarrassed that her surprise was so obvious. "I was starting to get sleepy. It's no wonder; this place is so deliciously quiet."

The shaggy-haired man smiled. "I wanted to see how it was going with the restoration of the paintings in the hunting lodge. I'm quite fond of them, and glad they're being restored."

"Are you the, uh, owner?" asked Celeste, rising from her chair, feeling as if she'd been caught by her boss while sleeping on the job. She had not met any of the family members who owned the estate, but had only interacted with business executors and assistants. But this man did have the look about him of a confident but approachable young heir.

"No, no, nothing of the sort," the man laughed, motioning for her to sit back down. "You needn't rise in my presence; I just work for the estate. My name's Peter." He stuck out his hand amiably. Celeste shook it. It was a pleasure, she noted to herself, to be able to speak simply in her native tongue with him; she understood German well, but spoke it slowly, clumsily, and as a result felt handicapped in her conversations with everyone else on the estate.

"I oversee operations and upkeep for several chateaus scattered through southern Germany, all owned by the same family — they are, as you might guess, extravagantly wealthy." He shared this last fact as if it were a humorous aside; one got the sense that money did not have a particularly high moral value in his eyes. "But, as I said, I love peering at those hunting paintings you're working on. How are they coming along?"

Celeste proceeded to tell him about the slow-but-steady progress of the restoration project. There were four large paintings, one on each of the four walls, which were aligned exactly with the four cardinal directions. The paintings were originally done in fresco at some point in the 18th century, with oil later applied in the 19th century, which meant her work now was a complex process of negotiating multiple layers of paint and past re-touchings. "The pictures themselves are exquisite," said Celeste, "and my goal is to preserve that strangely compelling *flat* feeling one gets from the images... that sense of looking through a window into a frozen scene from the past."

"That is lovely to hear, for those paintings really are special to me," replied Peter, seeming genuinely delighted by Celeste's appreciation for images that he had apparently spent a great deal of time looking at. "I am curious: what got you into painting in the first place?"

There was something about Peter's manner that made Celeste feel comfortable enough to speak freely, sharing her thoughts on art with an openness that she normally reserved for close friends. "Well, as a matter of fact, it was that same kind of mysterious flatness that these frescoes have; it's a quality I first noticed when I was a teenager, on a school field trip to one of the few art museums in Arizona. At some point I wandered off from the group, drawn down some lonely corridor to the medieval gallery, where there were very few people to be found. It seems to me now that I entered into a dream of some sort: I walked through a series of airy rooms upon whose gray walls were hung paintings framed in gold, depicting scenes which seemed to come from another world, so possessed were they of an interior stillness and reverence. There were free-standing glass cases scattered throughout the space as well, containing illuminated manuscripts: ancient books positioned in tilted cradles, opened to pages depicting biblical scenes in gold-leaf and lapis-lazuli splendor. I found myself particularly drawn, for reasons that are still unclear to me, to the background landscapes of these images: they seemed hazy, mysterious, with bare, bluish mountains against cloudless skies. They felt as if they were the glowing backdrops of a world filled with a pregnant silence, or perhaps it was that they seemed to be whispering something, but in a language I couldn't understand or fully hear. They were like scenes from a dream, and that night as I lay in my bed at home, I found myself returning to that gallery again and again in my mind. I went to the library the next day and got a book on medieval painting, and I suppose that marked the day my life in art begin."

Peter responded in a tone of unexpected somberness, as if she had touched on something of great personal significance to him. "I know what you speak of. That world you saw in the horizon of those paintings — it's the world we live in, but seen through the eyes of another age, seen in ways we have forgotten." He looked off wistfully in the distance, and spoke dreamily, as if reading lines off a far-off teleprompter. "I've caught glimpses of that vision, I think, in church, in the light falling on poplars, in the dancing flames of a campfire, in ground-mist slowly creeping along the ground at the outset of dawn."

Peter suddenly looked directly at Celeste with a wry smile, breaking off from his reverie. "Ah now, enough poetry — it's almost time for supper," he said, and as if in response, the dinner bell rang from the main building, echoing across the marble terrace and open lawn that lay between the mansion and the pool where they stood.

7.

Most evenings dinner was prepared for the entirety of the on-site staff at the estate, with people drifting in to eat at their leisure within a one-hour window. There were two long tables in the main dining hall, and people sat wherever they pleased. Celeste ate there some nights, while on others she took her dinner into the adjoining den, an airy room which was home to a grand stone fireplace and whose walls were covered with shelf upon shelf of books. On this particular evening, Celeste ate at the same table as Peter, though they did not get a chance to pick up the thread of their conversation.

Celeste found herself sitting next to the estate's head gardener, a jovial and well-spoken man whose face was furrowed with innumerable wrinkles, a legacy from decades of days spent working in the sun. His pale-blue eyes sparkled mischievously from under wild black eyebrows. Somehow or other the conversation turned to the forest, and the gardener regaled her with an overview of the deep history of the woodland: the estate tract was a tributary of the Black Forest, whose impressive sprawl was merely a vestigial fragment of the still-grander Hercynian Forest, which in times of antiquity had stretched unbroken from Switzerland to Romania.

The gardener led the conversation, which flowed freely despite the fact that Celeste's German was halting at best and some turns of phrases the gardener used eluded her entirely. The gardener did not seem to mind, but appeared quite content to hold forth on a subject near to his heart, and Celeste was quite captivated by what he shared.

"Pliny the Elder spoke of it, he did: a gloomy forest filled with birds whose feathers shone like fires at night. Julius Caesar spoke of the 'Hercynia Silva' — I take it you've read the *Gallic Wars* — as an immense wilderness filled with aurochs, elk, unicorns... 'The endless forests of Germania' were part of a super-forest enfolding within its reaches the Silva Carbonaria and the Ardennes."

The gardener paused and looked out one of the tall windows into the evening darkness.

"Strange isn't it, that this land of lost time, this mist-shrouded relic of a fertile past, should in later centuries garner a reputation as the clock-making capital of the world? Strange and yet fitting." He turned back to Celeste. "Have you been to the Clock Museum in Furtwangen yet?"

Celeste smiled and shook her head no. She replied, in grammatically wobbly German, that she would like to. The old gardener smiled, the lines in his face crinkling even more, looking as weathered and kindly as a fallen apple shriveled by the sun.

8.

The following day passed uneventfully, Celeste working on the restoration in the morning and going for a long walk in the afternoon. She did not return to the forest that day, but instead decided, on a whim, to walk down the main road that was the estate's only entrance and exit. It was long and stately, and though made of unpaved dirt, it was remarkably well-kept; the sun-bleached earth was pressed down so tight that it actually appeared smoother and cleaner than most roads of paved tarmac. Colonnades of tall, dignified pines, looking venerable and vaguely patrician, flanked the road on either side, their branches looming dark against the electric blue of the depthless sky. Clouds hung sleepily above the earth, their underbellies incandescent, as the sun gradually traced an arc across the sky. Afternoons like this, Celeste thought to herself, hold the kind of beauty that led the philosophers of earlier centuries to formulate their conceptions of the sublime.

The next morning, Celeste was working in the lodge, concentrating on the varying pattern of colors which comprised the painted foliage of the tree-line in the background of one of the hunting scenes, when Peter gave a friendly rap on the open door, announcing himself before he strode in. Celeste smiled and waved, starting to put down her paintbrush.

"Oh no, no, no — I do not mean to interrupt. I just wanted to pop by and take a look at how things were going," he said, and with his hands clasped behind his back he began to slowly walk around the room, quietly looking up at the paintings with a subdued smile upon his lips. Celeste continued the process of lightly applying viridian paint to a grassy field.

"I enjoyed talking with you the other day," Peter remarked softly as he strolled along. "And I see that these paintings do have something of the quality you encountered in your first experience with art: the intimation of a mysterious background." Peter was quiet for a while, gazing up admiringly at the verdant scenes above. "What I love most about the paintings in here, I think, is how Edenic they are."

Celeste paused her work. "Yes, they are certainly idyllic," she agreed, looking thoughtfully at the field before her.

Peter stopped in the center of the room, turning slowly in place to take in a panoramic view of all the walls. "You know, I have a pet theory that there are two ancestral themes in all art, only two: Eden and Fall. When you look through that framework, most works quickly sort themselves out quite easily. Edward Munch's 'The Scream' — obviously about the Expulsion. Watteau's paintings of soirées in endless rococo gardens: a rather dandy and debauched interpolation, yes, but reaching for Eden nonetheless. Caspar David Friedrich's work: overgrown ruins and landscapes swathed in mist — a fallen world in search of the lost paradise. Your Hudson River Valley painters" — Peter motioned toward Celeste, as if gesturing at her Americanness — "Eden all over. Jackson Pollock: perhaps Eden, perhaps Fall, perhaps Fall groping for Eden. Mark Rothko's final works" — here, Peter grew suddenly somber, a shadow of sorrow seeming to pass over his face, as if his own story had at some point brushed against that of Rothko's — "the work of a man staring over the precipice, straight into the abyss of the Fall, not seeing any hope of redemption."

"What about non-Western art? Chinese art?" asked Celeste.

"Well, for one: neither Judaism nor Christianity are 'Western' religions. Golgotha is in Jerusalem, not

Athens or Rome. Remember Abraham standing below the starry host of a glittering near-Eastern sky. And besides: Eden is the Eden of all peoples, the garden that lies at the beginning of all history."

Here Peter paused, and then added with a smile, re-summarizing his thesis as he had been taught to in grade-school essays: "Two themes, two themes only: Eden and Fall."

Celeste was quiet for a while. "I want to think about that for a while," she said. "It's certainly a novel conception."

"Oh, I wouldn't call it *novel* really," Peter said bashfully, playfully rocking on his heels.

"Well," Celeste observed, "novel for the art school I went to. Did you study art in school?"

"No, I studied economics. But after finishing university, I spent some time in Switzerland, at a kind of theological-philosophical commune called L'Abri; it's an alpine retreat center of sorts, a place where one can think deeply about the kinds of things one doesn't get a chance to when studying business."

"What led you to managing estates as you do now?"

Peter smiled. "That, I must say, is a rather long and winding story I will spare you. But in any case, I now find myself holding a position where I get to spend time in some of the most beautiful parts of my country. I get to see a lot of picturesque vistas, and get to ensure the estate staff are taken care of, and I have plenty of time to read and go on strolls. All in all, I'm pleased with the situation. Speaking of which" — here he glanced at his wristwatch — "it's time for me to go. I don't want to distract you any longer, and I'm supposed to be meeting with the groundskeeper to talk about herbicides." And with a prompt little bow, Peter left the room.

Alone once more, Celeste listened to the soft sound her paintbrush made with each stroke upon the wall. She liked speaking with Peter, she thought to herself, in part because he spoke English so well, which meant that she didn't need to embarrass herself by trotting out her fragmented German. But more than that, she enjoyed his presence because he didn't feel like he was trying to hit on her or impress her, or assert social dominance in the conversation — all tendencies which she had seemed to frequently encounter in men. Peter felt instead like a man who held within himself an incandescent joy, one which couldn't help but bubble up in casual conversation. His enthusiasm for art was, she reflected, a welcome change from the attitudes of many people she had encountered in art school, who seemed more interested in using aesthetic theories as a form of leverage or social currency than in seeing paintings as part of the larger fabric of the world.

Meditating upon the flat grassy field in front of her and the conversation's references to verdant scenes of Eden put Celeste in a mind to revisit the forest that afternoon. Perhaps this time, she thought, she might find the northern fence.

9.

The clouds were especially picturesque that day, hanging over the sky in flamboyantly puffy configurations, towering like cotton massifs above the diminutive earth. The moon was visible, even though it was early afternoon; it floated in cerulean depths, a portent of the evening to come. I wonder why the moon sometimes appears in the day like that, Celeste wondered to herself as she crossed the sunlit lawn, breathing in the intoxicating perfume of fresh-cut grass — the lively scent of growing things, of chlorophyll running through a trillion tiny plant veins.

As she passed a long, finely trimmed hedge which bounded the north end of the lawn, a phalanx of crows unexpectedly burst forth, sharp and sudden as lightning, soaring up from behind the belt of shrubbery and wheeling away into the limitless blue of the sky. Celeste paused a moment to look at them, then took the path heading straight into the forest.

The woods were dusky and vast, and she once more had the sensation of entering an enormous storehouse. A vista of endless upright trunks stood before her, looking to Celeste like a constellation of standing stones upon some silent British moor. She loved it here, in the dim, damp hallways of the forest.

She trotted along the path at a brisk pace, light cascading through the entwined boughs as if through gauze, while occasional breaks in the canopy of leaves allowed singular rays of sunshine to pass through, collecting in luminous yellow pools upon the forest floor. Celeste noticed occasional bright flashes, spurts of fluttering motion, off in one of those distant shafts of light. She peered forward, and realized it was a pair of butterflies dancing about. Their erratic motions, which seemed to be tracing circular hieroglyphs upon the air, touched a particular chord of memory, plucking a richly resonant tone, reverberating with the textures and sensations of childhood; in the space of a moment, she recalled the moths she had encountered growing up in southern Arizona: hawkmoths and tiger moths, silkmoths and sack-bearers, smoky moths and leopard-moths, clear-wings, burnets, and prominents, and the small, pale yucca moth, whose short-lived life serves to pollinate the yucca plant which in turn nurtures the moth's young. In a split second, Celeste relived countless nights watching the soundless fluttering of ghostly wings in the halide light of the back porch, and the dizzy, rococo paths those moths would trace in the black air. She remembered her father telling her tales of the butterflies he had caught as a boy in Brazil when accompanying his own father on surveying trips through the southern state of Amazonas, and Celeste recalled the awestruck hush with which he spoke of the translucent glass wings of *Haetera piera*, the amber phantom.

There had been a time in Celeste's life when she'd thought she might become a lepidopterist (no doubt part of the draw was the sheer pleasure to be had in the satisfying click and roll of that word upon the tongue: *lepidopterist*) — or as her mother preferred to say, "a butterfly hunter." In the summer before 9th grade, months before the autumnal field trip in which she became enamored with painting, Celeste collected enough moths and butterflies to fill a small glass shadow box, gently pushing pins through those filament-thin bodies with their exquisitely etched wings, so frail and yet so resilient.

It's strange, Celeste observed, the specific memories that rise unbidden at times, floating up from the stores of memory like buoyant flotsam from the hold of a sunken ship, bobbing to the surface of black, surging waters. With piercing clarity she recalled sitting in the backseat of the family station wagon in the heat of that same summer of 1963, reading a book called *The Aurelian* — a cheap paperback her mom had picked up for her from a drugstore spinner rack because the cover featured butterflies. It was a science-fiction novel about a butterfly specialist sent on a top-secret mission to explore a planet full of butterflies just discovered in Alpha Centauri. As Celeste read silently in the backseat, her mom and brother had sat in the front, and on the radio the song "Runaway" by Del Shannon was playing — a song whose organ solo always struck Celeste as having a strange, wild feel to it; something about it reminded her of mercury, the way that you could break a household thermostat and hold the glimmering, silver blob in your hands, letting it slide across the furrows of your palm, break into metallic rivulets, and then perpetually rejoin itself; it felt close, familiar, and yet also distant, otherworldly, something not of the earth.

Now, at twenty-three years old, Celeste considered it strange that this memory, from only ten years ago, seemed as if it were part of a distant past, a lost plateau of childhood she was now separated from and could only look on from across a great, nameless chasm.

10.

Immersed deep within the woods, Celeste cut a willowy figure in her brown turtleneck and blue jeans. All around her were the somber figures of immense trees, with shaggy masses of ivy clinging to their lower trunks like verdant beards and long-dead tendrils of vine running upwards and entwining themselves around their branches, and at the end of those many-forking arms, profusions of pine needles in dark green with bright chartreuse tips. The forest floor was bejeweled with small white flowers — perhaps edelweiss, she noted with a smile, recalling the gilded dream of the Von Trapps that had unfurled before her in an Arizona theater years ago, though she knew that the elevation was not high enough here for that flower to grow.

"The Black Forest," Celeste softly said aloud as she followed the winding dirt path. Letting her mind pleasantly drift where it would, she thought about the tone in which Peter had spoken of Rothko's later paintings, those slabs of unrelenting darkness, with their seemingly obdurate refusal to yield their meaning. Flat abysses, they brought to Celeste's mind the great abyss that yawned in the center of the country in which she walked: the black cancer that had overtaken Germany thirty years ago with a voracious desire to consume the flesh of other nations, an evil whose stubborn reality seemed to leave contemporary Germany speechless. It seemed to Celeste that modern societies lacked a framework for understanding how the horrors of history could exist alongside the beauty and ordinariness of every-day life, and so these nightmares were left undealt with and simply hung there unacknowledged, like black clouds. America too, had this darkness: the original sin of slavery whose legacy, rather than evaporating with emancipation, instead festered, growing in darkness like mold in a midnight cellar.

Celeste thought of the summer of 1969, only three years ago but already cemented in her generation's collective memory as some sort of milestone: in her mind, it was a cultural moment summed up in the vision of a futuristic ship launching into space, glittering white against the blue sky while many leagues below, American cities burned, and billow-ing black smoke rose from inner-city streets.

11.

After a time, Celeste came to an unexpected clearing. The trees gave way to a circular patch of grass, in the center of which stood a transparent structure that shone in the sun like a multifaceted crystal shard, though it was covered in wrack and ivy. It was a greenhouse gone to ruin, Celeste realized, one of the largest greenhouses she'd ever seen, consisting of a huge central dome with two rectangular transepts extending in either direction, all in all running the length of a football field. The structure consisted of clear glass, gone slightly greenish with time, with an elaborate metalwork frame which formed an ornate latticework of repeating patterns and ornamental curves. The framework had originally been painted white but was chipped away in many places now, revealing the steel beneath it, and some of the glass windows were broken in places.

For the most part though, the greenhouse appeared undisturbed, as if it had simply, quietly been given over to nature. Celeste had seen buildings fall into ruin which looked like they had died in great distress, or tragically fallen on hard times, but this building felt different: it seemed to radiate a serene sense of abandonment, as if it was joyously surrendered to its slow reclamation by the forest, as if that were its true purpose all along.

A glass door on the side of one of the transepts stood ajar, and Celeste entered through it slowly and with great care, as if she were entering an archeological dig whose dust should not be disturbed. The floor, originally of tightly packed earth, was now a world of grass, flowers, mushrooms, and moss. A many-tentacled colossus of ivy was in the early stages of the process of enveloping the entire building, its creepers running up and down the walls and ceiling. A row of trees ran in a straight line along the full length of the transept. They were of varying heights and girths, and a few of them brushed up against the ceiling; one or two had actually broken the glass in their perpetual ascent heavenward.

Celeste gazed calmly on the trees as they stood in the honeyed light, and saw that many of them held orbed fruit within their leafy recesses. This was, she realized, the site of an orangerie — a building expressly designed for growing exotic fruit trees and flora, the sealed glass providing a microclimate in which they could flourish. She imagined this conservatory in its heyday: men and women dressed in cream-colored formal attire, following the fashions and customs of an earlier time, strolling through a stifling hothouse world filled with row upon row of orange trees in blossom, perhaps alongside palm trees whose great leaves would occasionally brush the faces of visitors; she imagined the nostrils of members of the gentry dilating involuntarily as they stepped inside the glasshouse and first took in the equatorial scents which lay heavy upon the air.

In the center of the abandoned structure stood a large rounded basin of stone, the sides of which were rimed with a mossy scum, and the bottom of which was filled with a puddle of brackish black water. This pool likely once held water lilies or lotus flowers, the exotic centerpieces of a self-contained, semi-tropical dream. The whole place made Celeste think of etchings she had seen of London's Crystal

Palace in its heyday: a lost world of Victorian exotica and proto-futurist dreams, of blinding naïveté and sublime longing. She could imagine a Gilded Age plutocrat standing in here with a cigar and top hat, looking approvingly up and down at this attempt at a hermetic Eden.

12.

There within the hush of the glass atrium beside the still pool, Celeste bent down to pick up a shard of glass, which appeared to have fallen from the ceiling when a tree branch had finally wrestled its way through the atrium's top. The tree in question had raised its shaggy crown over the top of the building who knows how many years ago, and Celeste imagined the sudden crashing sound that must have broken the silence of this huge room the moment, night or day, the roof was pierced, and she pictured this translucent shard falling dully to the earth.

Celeste had heard once in a high school chemistry class that glass was actually a liquid that moved at an unimaginably slow rate, so that over the centuries, a pane of glass would gradually drift downward in its frame, growing thicker at the bottom of the sill, as could be observed in stained-glass windows. At the time, it had seemed to her that this couldn't possibly be true, but then again, her science teacher had said it, so she assumed he knew what he was talking about. Then in college, Celeste learned that this claim was in fact incorrect: glass was actually considered an amorphous solid, and there were other reasons for the observed thickness at the bottom of stained-glass windows. Reflecting on this later, she found herself wondering whether the varied man-made taxonomies for many things in the world — liquid and solid; phylum, genus, and species — were similar elaborate theories masquerading as facts, mere heuristics wearing the august robes of timeless truth. She believed in objective reality, certainly, but it seemed to her that the modern mind had overestimated its understanding of that reality.

Slowly turning around in a complete circle, Celeste surveyed the lay of the conservatory; it was, she realized, arrayed like a compass, with entrances to the north and south and arms extending east and west. Through the glass, the northern wall of the forest rose, brooding and regal. Cocking her head northeast, Celeste gazed out at the distant horizon; somewhere, many miles hence, lay far-away Russia, hoary and vast, the terrain growing colder and colder as one traveled in its direction, toward endless steppes and tundras stretching limitlessly away into the distance. She pictured Leningrad — the former St. Petersburg in its temporary Soviet disguise — right at this very moment, immersed in a swirl of glistening snowflakes descending from immense leaden clouds.

And then, conversely, Celeste turned southwest, and envisioned herself moving rapidly in that direction, rushing along cerulean seas, eventually approaching gold-yellow beaches with translucent blue bays and murky water-forests of silent mangroves, and farther still, across the great lap of North America, the dusky streets of her Arizona hometown. Farther still, she imagined the wind-bent trees adorning the coast of Big Sur, rising like twisted monuments beside a curtain of stately, silent redwoods, as frigid Pacific waves hurled themselves upon the rock cliffs of California's western edge, continuing their long, slow task of devouring the continent's side.

Big Sur. She'd been there three times, once with her family and then twice in college. She associated the place with the smell of woodsmoke and salt air, of clary sage and patchouli; with late-night talks around a campfire, and glimpses of eccentrically constructed cedar cabins hidden between trees; with the phantasmagoric covers of Yes LPs, and the voices of Joni Mitchell and Bob Dylan drifting from car radios; with long-haired, dreamy-eyed art students, and rising funnels of woodsmoke wafting up into starlit forest eaves, and dog-eared paperback copies of Tolkien rolling around in the backseats of beat-up Volkswagens, and hanging over it all the semi-apocalyptic, semi-utopian feeling of creative possibility and dark inexorability that seemed to envelop the West Coast in a thick haze during those years.

Celeste recalled one late afternoon, driving in a van with four other students from art school, pulling over on the edge of Highway One, stepping out and standing upon the very cusp of North America, gazing out along the rolling expanse of wine-dark water. One of her friends, a musician and painter named Darien, had nudged her and pointed to a tiny speck way off in the distance. It was a boat, with a shimmering wake trailing behind it, and Darien told her, in a lowered voice, as if to signify that he was sharing an intimate secret, that once he'd been to a party in Los Angeles on David Crosby's legendary yacht *The Mayan*, anchored off Newport Beach. Crosby wasn't even there that night, but the ship itself was a thing of beauty, said Darien: forty-five feet of embodied hippie idealism and nautical daydreams. The interior was filled with exquisite wood paneling, tasseled rugs, Persian throw pillows, and the like; walking around, you could imagine Crosby simply clambering onboard whenever the fancy took him, then sailing off into the soft pastels of an early morning dawn, taking leave of the hidebound world of the shore — the world of money, numbers, evening news, and the encroaching sense that civilization was just circling the drain — and gliding away into the sun-kissed bosom of the ageless Pacific.

That was the exact phrase Darien had used: *the ageless Pacific.* Celeste wasn't sure if he had told her this story because it had genuinely come to mind as they stood there gazing at the sea, as light poured down from a crack in the clouds, or whether he had merely been seizing an opportune moment to impress her with a tale of ostensibly hobnobbing with the rich and famous. Standing now alone in the depths of the Black Forest, Celeste remembered that later that particular evening Darien had hit on her, his hands fumbling their way around her shoulder as their group all sat around a campfire, their young, uncreased faces illumined by the warm yellow flame-light, a glowing circle vignetted within the night world of trees and stars, far from the city. She recalled Darien leaning over clumsily to kiss her neck, and her pushing him away with an uneasy laugh. A few days later, as their group stopped for gas on the way out of San Francisco, she and Darien were alone for a moment, and he sullenly turned to her and said, "You're pretty uptight, you know that?" She didn't know quite what to say, and was relieved when someone came back into the car and giddily dumped a load of gas station snacks onto the floor, laughing and loudly exhorting them to eat up and grow strong. Celeste didn't really speak much to Darien again; they had never been close leading up to the trip, but were merely in the same friend group, and his attempt at getting close to her felt like one of a string of inarticulate grasps at female attention; though she did observe that most of his other attempts had been successful.

In her interactions with Darien leading up to his clumsy advance, she had noticed a dynamic which she'd encountered before: a feeling with certain boys that when they showed romantic interest in her, they were unintentionally looking through her at something else, some projection for which she served as a locus; some vision of empyrean mystery or embodied sensuality. Strange, the way men and women turn each other into ciphers, into totems of love eternal, or vessels in which to encode a set of ineffable longings, symbols of something they've always sensed missing in themselves, attempting to fashion from a human being a gilded peg upon which to hang suppositions of what it is to feel alive.

13.

Of course, thought Celeste, everyone has their own strategies for managing and sublimating inscrutable longings. While she was in high school in Arizona, her older brother Fernão and his buddies used to spend their free time tearing out the interiors of their junky cars and installing roll cages into the frames before putting the insides back together with added padding. Those were the cars they'd take out racing on hot nights, heading out to lonely desert roads and driving as fast as they could stomach, then intentionally taking turns when they knew full well there was no way they could handle at those speeds, bracing themselves at just the right angle. *Controlled crashes*, they called it. Celeste remembered Fernão telling her what the experience felt like; he said it was like leaving the earth for a moment in which you become so acutely aware of the fact that you are alive that you can almost sense the individual blood cells throbbing in your veins, and when a climactic turn comes and the car begins to shudder and then turn over as it veers off the road, sometimes you hear the screaming of metal and the squealing of tires, but other times the lead-up to a crash is weirdly muted, as if the whole scene were playing out silently before the shadowy figures of the watching mountains and Joshua trees.

Fernão and his friends did get hurt at times, occasionally pretty badly, but often they stepped out of those crashes without a scratch; the roll cages did their job. When Celeste's father found out about what they were doing, he begged Fernão to stop. She remembering hearing them having it out in the garage one night, while the cicadas thrummed loudly outside; the men's voices escalated in volume, finally coming to a crescendo when her father began yelling in Portuguese, switching from English to his native tongue in the heat of passion, proclaiming that one of Fernão's friends would be dead within the year. His prediction came true later that summer when Jonny Alvarez's Dodge Coronet turned over seven times. Fernão was the first one to find him, running up to the smoking wreckage of the car to see Jonny lying pinned in the driver's seat, impaled by a bar from the twisted roll cage, and staring up at the star-pierced sky as his last breaths came in ragged gasps. With that, the teenagers' ritualized game of night thrills ended.

The years had passed, and Fernão was a family man now, but Celeste knew that he still drove out some evenings to lonely stretches of highway to race by himself. No roll cages or sharp turns this time, simply a sensation of speed: an escape velocity. He confided to her what it was like to open up on the highway on clear nights, to floor the gas and feel the dizzy rush of acceleration as the Milky Way wheeled overhead; he said he knew it was irresponsible, with a wife and two daughters at home who depended on him, but at certain times, something came over him, and when it did, nothing else seemed to matter.

14.

"What are you doing in here?" a female voice rang out in the glass atrium, its tone not unkind. Celeste spun around to see its source. An old woman, tall and stately even from afar, was standing at the far side of the transept opposite. She must have appeared from around the side of one of the overgrown orange trees.

Celeste waved and smiled. "Just out for a walk. I didn't know there was anyone else here."

The woman drew closer, the hint of a smile playing upon her pursed lips. She walked with a light step, and as she came near, Celeste got a better look at her. She wore a light fur coat, her head was wrapped in a green scarf with white flowers, and her face, though lined with age, was beautiful. She looked like she could have been a princess in some earlier epoch, with her high cheekbones and glistening dark eyes. Celeste could imagine her slowly stepping onto a marble pedestal from a carved, high-backed throne before a waiting court.

"I come here every so often," the woman began, "but I haven't bumped into anyone else here in a long time. My name's Anise." She held out her right hand, and Celeste took it. As they shook, Celeste noticed a flash of light coming from Anise's ring finger; upon it was a silver band with an amber orb upon the bezel. Anise noticed Celeste noticing it, and she held her hand up, the amber gem catching the light; within it was a tiny white flower, its five frail petals suspended within the luminous resin.

"Star jasmine," Anise explained. "A family heirloom of sorts."

"It's lovely," said Celeste politely.

"It's supposed to be ageless, forever preserved in the golden sap of a long-gone tree. The ancient Athenian general Nicias said that amber was the dew of the sun, carried from the soil to the sea before being cast up upon the shores of Germania."

Celeste was unsure how to respond to this. Anise had a strangely regal way of speaking, but there was also a kind of sad lilt to her speech, as if she were used to not being understood.

Celeste gestured at the expansive glass structure in which they stood. "What happened to this place?"

Anise gazed up at the roof. Her skin was stretched thin upon her face, and strangely seemed both olive-dark and yet pale; upon it, Celeste could see the faint blue etchings of the blood vessels beneath. She must have been at least seventy, Celeste thought to herself. Through the clear glass above them, a vast flock of birds could be observed, surging and pulsing in inscrutable, weirdly magnetic mathematical patterns through the open fields of the sky. Celeste recalled reading somewhere that such a movement was called a murmuration, an appropriately poetic-sounding term for a phenomenon which, like the dawn chorus, seemed to belong to a secret realm of birds, filled with dances and songs known only to themselves and God.

"I used to visit this place when I was younger, and it too was in full flower then. It belonged to a family around here, all of whom are now passed. But it was a great greenhouse, absolutely thrumming with well-kept life, a miniature world unto itself." Anise smiled, her eyes sparkling as scenes from summers long gone passed before her vision; she was internally viewing a parade of youthful splendor. "But history has a way of sweeping away such miniature worlds."

"Do you live nearby then?" asked Celeste, curious without wanting to appear intrusive.

"Not too far, a little village over that way." Anise gestured to the east. As she did so, she began stepping backward, as if she were a figurine in a cuckoo clock mechanically retreating into its wooden chalet. "And in fact, I should be getting back. Maybe I'll see you again," she remarked upon reaching the lintel of the door. She then turned around and trotted out on her way.

Celeste watched as the woman walked up to the southern edge of the forest, then disappeared into the enfolding embrace of the firs, their branches softly swaying in a gentle breeze.

The atmosphere inside the observatory was quiet and still; Celeste felt as if she were standing inside a painting. An invisible rivulet of moving air stirred the top of one of the orange trees, and as it rustled slightly in response, a single mantis-green leaf fell from it, glimmering as it spun over and over upon its slow voyage downwards, landing silently upon the lush expanse of plant matter that carpeted the atrium.

Celeste realized it was high time she headed back to the estate, and turned and left by the same door she'd entered. Outside, the grass was studded with gentians blooming an iridescent blue, the vaulted sky was darkening ever so gradually, and the late afternoon breeze was growing stronger, carrying upon its chill breath the rumor of a coming storm. Celeste found the path leading homewards, and, stepping back into the shaded canopy of thickly interlaced branches, she began her return journey.

15.

Lying in bed that night, Celeste gazed at the ceiling of her room, which was painted a light cream color that, in the darkness of evening, appeared as a flat gray expanse. There in the still silence, waiting for sleep to overtake her, she recalled a moment from the same family road trip in which she'd first seen Big Sur, on the way back, when they had stopped for the night in a Las Vegas hotel. It happened to be the night before Celeste turned thirteen. Twelve years old, she'd lain awake in bed and gazed up at the ceiling, thinking that the popcorn stucco looked like an upside-down moonscape, all cratered and white, a stark and barren geography. Thirteen, she'd thought to herself then. She'd remembered how, upon turning ten, she'd thought it marvelous to have racked up a full decade of life in the world. Now at midnight the clock of her life was to advance yet another year, to mark thirteen years on the planet Earth.

Young Celeste had been utterly mesmerized by Vegas itself. There was something weirdly timeless about all those unapologetically lurid casinos — with their enclosed worlds of recycled air, lit perpetually by artificial suns. They offered interior fantasy-lands where it was neither night nor day, where plastic shrubbery sat unchanging, gathering dust, beside miles and miles of red carpeting and mirrored ceilings; where the songs of lounge singers floated down empty hallways, mingling with the incessant trills of gaming machines crowned with pulsing neon. Those spaces seemed timeless in the sense that they were profoundly bound to a specific moment in time — they so thoroughly embodied a certain point in 20th-century America, and presented such deeply strange simulations of a decadent Western dream, that they felt disconnected from history itself, like a cul-de-sac in the stream of time, as fruitless and sterile as the artificial plants and hollow simulations of Paris, Rome, nature, and love which filled the city itself. In such a place, Celeste could envision many a tourist sitting contentedly within the cocoon of a hotel room, freed from the concerns of the present and of responsibilities to family, community, and God, instead feeling encased in the placelessness of the desert, in the anonymity of a glowing mirage, preparing to head downstairs and spend an evening wandering alone through the sprawling corridors of this vast, interconnected complex, this doomed El Dorado of the West, while off in the distance, leaden walls of cloud, thick with water, steadily rolled over waiting desert plains.

The next day, after spending the morning walking around town gawking at artificial wonders and lunching at the perfunctory all-you-can-eat buffet, with its multicolored array of food from around the world and under the sea, the newly-teenaged Celeste and her family drove back home to Arizona. She and her brother sat in the backseat and stared out the dusty car windows as the sun drowned the world in molten gold. They rode past flat stretches of desert interspersed with tourist traps and gas stations, and when they passed through small towns, they'd gaze at the local restaurants, tiny post offices, and modest main streets. The late afternoon gently faded into night, and the cobalt sky, flat yet intimating limitless depth, acting as an immense screen between Earth and the celestial palace in which the planet spun, deepened into a shadowy violet and became translucent, revealing the stars in their countless flocks.

It was a long drive, with stretches of darkness punctuated by the bright signs of service stations and front-lit billboards. Around dinnertime they stopped at a fast-food joint whose canted roof featured a monumental neon sign, its unearthly glow beckoning travelers off the highway like the siren of some electric reef, glimmering with the promises of a consumer age. Looking at the towering sign as she munched on hot french fries, Celeste had realized, though she could not fully articulate it, that Las Vegas was not merely a place in Nevada, but an elaborate and blatant outworking of an impulse which undergirded much of American culture.

And, a little over ten years later, as Celeste lay in a German bed examining this remembered view of the faraway American republic, it was with this thought that she dimly sensed the great doors of sleep opening up and ushering her in, her eyelids fluttering into stillness.

16.

The next morning, Celeste continued her work upon the lodge paintings. Having finished the southern and eastern friezes, she now turned to the western. It featured the image of a great white mountain towering up into the sky like a jagged tooth, with a small expedition of mountain climbers upon its western face, which was drenched in golden sunlight. Off in the distance of the painting, a shadowy herd of storm clouds were rolling in. Looking at the scene, one could almost sense the dampness in the air, the drop in barometric pressure upon one's skin.

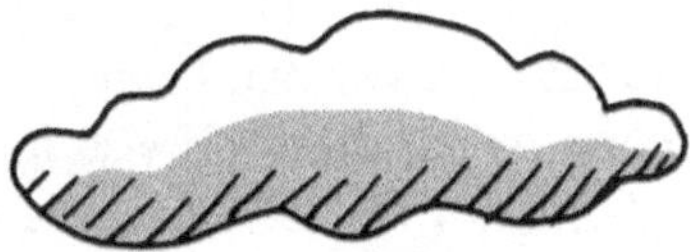

When working on the restoration, Celeste sought to focus on the task at hand — maintaining the integrity of the image and the vibrance of the original colors — without necessarily thinking about the people who had originally painted and commissioned the piece, their motivations and designs, their lives and preoccupations. But now she did let her mind drift to centuries earlier: how many nights, she wondered, did the original mansion owner gaze up at this very same painting, illumined by flickering flames upon the hearth while rain hammered the roof and lightning lit up the shadowy hills outside, momentarily framing the bent shapes of trees in a blazing blue?

Glancing up at the portion of roof above the stone fireplace, Celeste saw a tell-tale darkening of the upper wall and ceiling, the smoky residue of countless fires. Doubtless that roof had been scrubbed over and over, like a palimpsest, but the cumulative memory of burning wood could never be fully erased from the place.

That afternoon, Celeste went walking in the forest once more. There was a hint of chill in the air, and so she wore a heavy poncho over her customary jeans and ribbed-neck sweater. Under the poncho, she felt secure and at home; it was like an old, well-loved blanket to her. She'd had it since she was a teenager, having bought it on a family trip to Mexico, and it had accompanied her on many trips since.

As was her custom, she began in a northward direction, with the vague but not especially pressing goal of reaching the northern fence line. She noticed rain-swollen clouds gathering upon the eastern horizon, and in the back of her mind she made a note not to be out too long lest she get soaked. But that mental note was soon filed away and forgotten, for it was an especially lovely day, one in which the colors and contours of the natural world seemed particularly vivid and sharply drawn, fresh as if all the earth had been made anew the preceding night; Celeste found herself ineluctably drawn into a reverie, walking lightly along the forest path and feeling as if she were hovering a few inches above the ground.

It was with a start that the reality of getting caught in a summer rainstorm came rushing back into Celeste's mind. She found herself standing once more in the open clearing before the glass greenhouse, having just emerged from the cloistral gallery of the forest, and the damp smell of coming rain flooded her nostrils, rising from the ground with an earthy pungency. The sky above was a mottled wall of bluish-gray cloud, and a moment later, she felt stray droplets of water, fat and cold, beginning to fall here and there. She turned and headed back into the forest, but as she did she heard from afar the rushing sound of a heavy rain descending in a sheet upon the terrestrial world. There was a white flash, followed a few seconds later by a booming crack of thunder which rattled the earth. Celeste quickened her pace.

Within a few minutes, the woods were a sodden microcosm of dripping boughs and black mud, and Celeste was soaked to the skin. The flashes of lightning continued, and the sky grew steadily darker, as if night had decided to steal in upon the world several hours early that day. In the mud and rain, she found it difficult to keep track of the serpentine trail, and soon enough she realized she had wandered off it. Turning back to where she thought the path was, she cursed the way the trees seemed to form a grid of endless corridors stretching off in all directions, the very quality which had so delighted her upon earlier strolls.

She somehow managed to find the path and continued farther upon it, yet after successfully following its twists and turns for another quarter mile, found herself again off course. She doubled back, but this time could not find any traces of the trail. The rain was relentless, and the forest dark. In frustration, Celeste slapped her heel down upon the mud, which let off a defensive squelch. She was lost at this point, and it was night-dark here in the shadow of the storm, and the wind was cold. She considered the possibility of simply standing under an obliging tree until the storm passed, but already she was beginning to shiver; her best bet was to head in the direction she took to be home. Striking out toward what seemed to be south, Celeste trudged onwards through the slanting rain.

17.

It became clear that Celeste had headed in the wrong direction when, unexpectedly, the trees parted before her and she stepped out onto the bare crest of a high hill. Looking to her left and right, she saw the woodland's edge extending far away in both directions, following along the ridge of the hill. Directly before her lay the sloping basin of a dim valley filled with rolling hills, at the center of which she could make out the inky-black silhouettes of several low buildings framed by the grayish darkness of open fields. In one of the structures, which looked like it was maybe a mile away, she could see several rectangles of golden light: the windows of a farmhouse. Deciding to make for the house to see if the owner would let her warm up and wait out the storm, Celeste began to carefully pick her way down the grassy slope, taking great care not to slip upon the soggy soil.

Her situation was physically unpleasant, yes, but Celeste found herself smiling nonetheless. Being lost out here reminded of her father; it was the sort of situation he seemed to have relished getting into when he was younger. When Celeste was growing up, her father had regaled her and Fernão with tales of the adventures of his youth, his time spent wandering the *sertão*, Brazil's northern hinterland, camping out in the open hills each night, beneath an unpolluted sky. He said the stars were so close there you felt you could touch them. He often waxed eloquent about Brazil — its people, its landscapes, its flora and fauna, its music and food — and in a sense his children had inherited a haunted longing for the country whence their blood had sprung. And yet they knew they would not be going back anytime soon. Celeste's father and mother had left Belo Horizonte shortly before Fernão was born because they sensed a storm brewing in the political atmosphere. From their new home in America, they followed Brazil's various government crises and successions from afar, and with the completion of the new capital, Brasília, in 1960, their family briefly considered moving back. Celeste recalled her father eagerly showing her images of that city's bold, swooping architecture, shining white amidst vast, uncluttered avenues beneath a widescreen, cloud-besotted sky. "*Venturis ventis*," he said in an excited hush, repeating the city's motto, "To the coming winds."

But the Nascimento family had already put down deep roots — friends, church, school, work — in the Arizona town to which they had emigrated, and so they tarried, and then Brazil's subsequent military coup permanently ended their hopes of return. Still, Celeste knew her father longed for the Brazil of his youth, for the people, for the endless backcountry, for the sight of the green mountain of Corcovado glistening in the early morning... America was now their home, yes, but the color of their skin, the traces of her parents' accents, the way Celeste and Fernão had been formed by a household representing a fusion of middle-class America and a microcosmic recreation of Brazilian culture — at times they could all feel the tension, the mismatch, between who they were and what they saw represented in television and movies. Celeste felt it, too, in the way her friends had little to no interest or understanding of the world south of the American border.

Presently, Celeste reached a small, low wooden fence at the edge of the farmhouse property. Stepping over it, she made her way toward the warm yellow light pouring from the farmhouse windows. In the distance, she could make out the dim shape of looming triangular structures, like pyramids, and wondered to herself what they might be. Fixing her attention back on the farmhouse, she could smell woodsmoke, and thought to herself that it must surely be one of the most comforting scents known to man.

18.

Celeste summoned the courage to walk up to what she took to be the front door, and, standing dripping upon the doorstep, rapped softly three times, then stepped back and waited. From within, she heard the creaking of someone getting up from an old chair, accompanied by the scuffle of paws scrambling upon floorboards — the sound of a dog roused from sleep by the movement of its owner. The door opened, the flickering orange light of the fireplace flooding out into the wet night air and falling in a glowing square upon the mud before the entrance.

The face that greeted Celeste was that of Anise, the woman from the greenhouse.

"Oh, h-hello again," Celeste stammered in surprise, in English.

Anise smiled, unperturbed, and motioned for Celeste to enter, replying also in English, "Come in, come in, it's wet outside!"

"I'm terribly sorry to bother you — I got caught in the storm; I'm completely soaked," said Celeste, stepping in out of the cold; within a few moments, her dripping sweater and jeans had formed little pools of water upon the worn wood floor.

"It's our pleasure to help," Anise said matter-of-factly, and quickly busied herself, grabbing a large woolen blanket from a hallway closet and a towel from another cupboard and giving them to the shivering Celeste. Anise then set a kettle of water upon the black cast-iron stove, which looked centuries old.

Wrapping herself in the comforting embrace of the big blanket, Celeste looked around the room. A fire was roaring heartily in a stone fireplace that dominated one corner of the room, and a modest wooden table stood at the far end of the room, which adjoined onto the kitchen; beside the table was a short wooden bookcase packed full of hardcovers in various languages. A center hallway led off into the other rooms of the house, and the whole place felt exactly as one would hope that a traditional-style dwelling in the Black Forest would feel: warm, weathered but clean, and cozily cheerful.

Anise beckoned Celeste to take a seat before the fire, drawing up a stout oak chair. Celeste nodded in gratitude and sat down. Anise bustled around the kitchen for a bit, and soon she and Celeste were both sitting before the fire, each holding a hand-made mug of spiced cider, Celeste wearing a kind of loose-fitting kaftan the woman had provided.

"Thank you again for your kindness," said Celeste. "I didn't expect to see you again — under these circumstances, in any case. I was on a walk; I ended up at the glasshouse again, in fact, and the storm took me by surprise."

"This storm," Anise motioned up toward the roof, which was thrumming with the falling of heavy rain, "won't be passing for some time, at least until midnight. It is best you stay the night here; my husband and I have a spare room, and would be happy to have you."

"That's so kind of you," said Celeste. She felt some-what reluctant to impose upon her host, but she also realized Anise was speaking sense; it would be unwise to try to make it back to the manor on a night like this. "I can't possibly repay you."

Anise smiled warmly. "I did my fair share of gala-vanting about and getting lost in the woods when I was your age, too. More than once did my friends and I find ourselves in the same position as you, soaked right through and in need of a warm fire and solid roof. Have you ever heard of the *Wandervögel* — the wandering birds?"

Celeste shook her head no, and took a sip of the piping cider, in which she could detect a warming hit of *kirschwasser*, the cherry brandy popular in the region.

"It was a youth movement here in Germany, many years ago. It reminds me of your generation now — the long-haired young bohemians I see photos of in the papers, the bright-eyed, unshaven American students who stream into Europe, on their way to see the world. When I was young, we too loudly extolled natural living, freedom, love. We too were unapologetically idealistic, beautiful, bare-faced, by turns somber and ridiculous, full of wild hopes. We tramped through the woods at night on extravagantly long hikes, carrying guitars and singing our hearts out, dreaming of a world without war, without boundaries. We too fumbled around with wild philosophies and each other's bodies; we were giddy about poetry and ideas, and we too saw all too clearly the hypocrisy of our forefathers."

Celeste watched Anise intently as she spoke; there was a quiet intensity to her voice, a strange lilt. It was as if she were poised on the brink of tears, as if she were at pains to hold herself back from falling into a great well of memory.

"That was the nineteen-twenties and thirties — and I saw what became of my fellow wandering birds, my wide-eyed companions. Some of them eventually became respectable bourgeoisie, as is to be expected. Some of them saw the rising tide, and fled or resisted. And some of them became the very architects of the dark age which stole in upon my country. I couldn't believe it myself when I saw it happen — the men and women with whom I had hiked up mountains and talked long into the night of love and art and high ideals — when I saw what they were capable of doing."

At this point, Anise felt silent for a time, and gazed off at a corner of the room. Celeste was quiet too.

After a time, Anise spoke again, without shifting her gaze from the wall. "I had thought that loving beautiful things made one good, but I was certainly disabused of that notion. I hope the people of your generation won't need to learn the same lesson, though I think you will."

Anise bowed her head for a moment, then abruptly seemed to perk up and changed her tone. "But tell me, what brings you to this little hamlet of ours?"

Celeste explained her restoration work and art school background, and the desire to see Europe that had led her here. Anise listened attentively, her eyes sparkling in the firelight; through Celeste, she seemed to be re-living what it was to be young, the rest of your life stretching out before you, a broad land of myriad paths and possibilities. Anise in her turn told Celeste a bit about her life — her two grown sons, now living in Munich, and how she and her husband had both grown up in this area of the Black Forest and moved away, but after living in many different cities, found themselves drawn back here, to spend their twilight years in the same village and manner of life as their ancestors. She spoke of the pleasures of gardening, of raising chickens, of quietly divesting oneself of the trappings of city life. She spoke of her frequent visits to the glasshouse, which evidently functioned for her as a makeshift memorial to her youth. Celeste could sense that Anise was intentionally speaking of pleasant things, consciously holding in check some well of internal darkness. Celeste thought once more that there seemed to be something regal about Anise's bearing, her composure; she was like a proud queen who had seen her kingdom's imminent fall fast approaching, but did not see it fit to countenance this knowledge.

After telling of her life, and asking Celeste more questions about hers, Anise finally got up and gently bowed toward Celeste. "We go to bed early around here," she explained, "so I'll prepare your room, just down the hallway. You're welcome to sit by the fire as long as you like."

Celeste thanked her again and Anise showed her where the guest room was, then excused herself for the evening. Celeste sat and gazed deep into the dancing yellow flames and glowing embers, listening to the satisfying crack and hum of burning logs — the tiny, muffled explosions of resin pockets within the grain giving way before the flames. Though it wasn't really that late at all, probably only seven or eight, Celeste felt her eyelids growing heavy. The fire seemed to have a soporific effect, and it was with effort that Celeste finally got up and drowsily made her way to her room, and there found a feathered bed with voluminous blankets and freshly laundered white sheets.

As she drifted off to sleep, Celeste dimly remembered a bedtime story that she had heard long ago, a fairy tale of twelve princesses who would go each night through a trapdoor in the floor of their bedroom, down a long mysterious passageway, and through groves of trees with silver, gold, and diamond leaves, until they finally came to a glittering underground lake. Boarding boats, the twelve princesses would cross the shimmering waters to a great hidden castle, where they partook in a grand ball, dancing until dawn. As a little girl, Celeste found herself taken with the weirdly beautiful imagery of castle spires rising over the surface of a subterranean lake; she found that detail of the story far more interesting than the rest of the plot, which concerned the unlikeable princesses and their attempts to thwart a series of would-be suitors who sought to discover their secret.

19.

Celeste could not remember ever having had a more satisfying night's sleep. She awoke in the soft splendor of a warm bed piled with blankets, and after a long, drawn-out stretch and yawn, rolled out of bed and found her clothes from last night dried and folded up neatly on a small wicker chair. There was a small window set high in the wall above her bed, and peering through it she saw the scene of a rural idyll which could easily have been a portal into an earlier century: chickens were pecking about in a grassy yard beside a low fence, and a man with an unkempt white beard sat on a wooden stool, milking a speckled cow, while off in the distance a wooden cart loaded with a tall pile of hay could be seen rolling along a deep-rutted road of dried mud. Above it all, the sky was a brilliant tapestry of rilled peach clouds, the edges of which glistened in the ascendant morning sun. Celeste pulled on her sweater and walked out to greet her host.

Out in the kitchen, Anise had prepared a breakfast of fresh cream, warm bread, berries, butter, and coffee, all laid out in a neat array upon the weathered wooden table. Celeste stumbled over her words in effusively thanking Anise for her hospitality.

Anise smiled. "Think nothing of it; it's our pleasure to have a guest for the evening. My husband wants to meet you, by the way. He's out milking the cow but will be in soon enough."

After a while, her husband came in, a burly bearded man in his sixties. He seemed to be one of those men who, rather than weakening with age, appear to grow stronger and more imposing with the years, like old oaks that grow tougher the more winters they endure. He bowed with a smile toward Celeste, introduced himself as Rolf, then took a seat at the table and began loading his plate with food.

"I hear you're doing renovation work at Fernweh," he said, with a twinkle in his eye. "I am quite fond of those paintings." Reading Celeste's surprised expression, he amiably explained: "I am friends with the estate gardener, and he tells me most everything that goes on on there; I've stayed in that hunting lodge several times, in fact. So tell me, how is the restoration coming along?"

"It's going well; I think I may be done in three weeks or so, barring any complications," said Celeste.

Rolf nodded approvingly, "Yes, that's good. It will be fine to see those paintings returned to what they were." He then proceeded to eat a hearty breakfast, scarcely saying a word but proceeding with an air of good humor that made the silence of the table feel relaxed rather than uncomfortable.

After Celeste finished her meal, she helped clear away the dishes and thanked her hosts once more. Rolf gave her directions for getting back to the manor-house, and he and Anise walked Celeste out the door to their garden gate, then bid her goodbye.

Alone again in the day-lit world, blinking in the sun, Celeste saw that the farmhouse she had stayed in was one of a series of structures stretching off into the green-and-gold haze of the valley. The pyramidal shapes she had dimly glimpsed the night before were in fact the forms of several imposing dwellings which lay spread out before her: great rustic structures with huge, sloping roofs like wide-brimmed hats. A few people could be seen moving about here and there, carrying wood or moving carts or simply going on walks. The whole vale was like an open-air museum, filled with the quiet sounds of a lifestyle that had been continuing on for hundreds of years, with men and women, children and animals, living among byre-dwellings with long, thatch-covered roofs that swept all the way down to the ground, surrounded on all sides by the silent eaves of the forest.

As she followed the path that led out of the valley and up the slope into the woodland, Celeste thought of what the gardener had told her about the Black Forest being the remnant of a far greater ancient woodland, and she realized this little village was a relic, too, in its own way, of another vanished world.

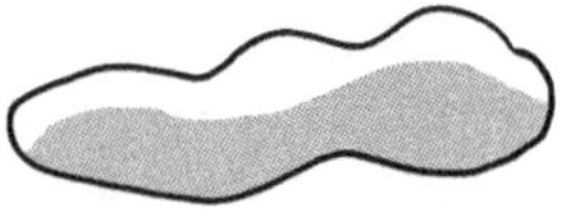

20.

Making her way back to the estate, wearing her warm, familiar poncho, Celeste delighted in the radiance of the rain-washed forest. The sun was out and beginning to warm the world; drops of water still fell from branches here and there, the foliage was clad in dew, and the earth was black and damp. Tiny battalions of slugs, snails, and worms had emerged after the previous night's downpour, and were canvassing the grass and ground, leaving behind telltale silvery trails which caught the fresh sunlight that streamed down through the light-filled leaves. The thick moss, which lay in rug-like patches along the forest floor and engirdled the trunks of trees, seemed to have grown thicker, deeper, overnight, and the air was filled with a pleasant, fertile redolence: the scent of growing things, of wet dirt and new life, of the rainbow after the flood. There could be heard a soft chattering of birds in the canopy overhead, and Celeste felt as if all living things around her were feeling a similar sense of joyous relief, of wordless celebration.

Rolf's instructions were to follow the westward path out of the village as it rose up the hill and plunged directly into the side of the forest; within a kilometer, he said, you would meet up with a larger path running north-south, at which point turning left would take you straight back to the estate. But after walking at least three kilometers, Celeste had not come across any other path, or even the hint of one. She paused, and looked back. Had there been, perhaps, a fork in the road she had missed? But no, her memory was clear on that point; she had gone straight along the path and encountered no divergences. Perhaps the north-south road had been swallowed up by vegetation since Rolf had last encountered it? That too struck Celeste as unlikely; Rolf seemed clearly to be the sort of man who intimately knew the highways and byways of the region, and who regularly traipsed around the woods that comprised his backyard — he would have duly noted if any of these local paths had been effaced.

It was hard to be worried though, for standing here in the greenish light of day, feeling the sun dry the earth, Celeste couldn't help but smile. She decided to follow the path farther; perhaps Rolf had underestimated the distance to the crossroads, and in any case, this path would no doubt eventually lead *somewhere*.

Ambling along, following the twisting and turning way through the forest, Celeste felt herself lapse once more into a reverie. The twittering songs of swallows echoed through the upper eaves of trees, and shafts of light fell across the path, illuminating motes of plant matter which floated along the air as if engaged in a slow, mysterious migration through the woodland. She passed through fragrant profusions of lilies-of-the-valley with their gently curving stalks upon which hung, like pendants, sprays of white bell-shaped flowers.

The canopy above seemed to grow more dense and tangled, and the light grew dimmer as Celeste walked deeper into the forest. Within this shadowy world, there seemed to be an exponential profusion of fungi and twisted roots, of ivy which clothed trees in a shaggy mantle. Celeste felt as if she had entered a grove within a grove, a gloomy corner of the woodland realm.

Then, with a turn of the road, the dim corridor of trees widened somewhat, revealing at the center of the green-shod floor a large pile of stones, which stood about ten-feet high and was overgrown with vines and a velvety moss. It was, she realized, the fireplace of a vanished home; at the center of the pile, an inset shelf of blackened stones indicated the hearth, bearing the shadow of ancient flames.

Celeste looked around her, in wonder that she was standing in the footprint of a former dwelling, of which all traces had disappeared except these stones robed in ivy.

It reminded her of the twelve-foot obelisk she had once seen in the White Sands desert of New Mexico, on a road trip she and her father had taken in 1966. That obelisk, a pyramidal monument of cobbled lava rock, marked the site of the first-ever test of a nuclear bomb. Standing before it in the glaring light of the midday sun, surrounded by other tourists milling about and snapping photos before this strange artifact, seventeen-year-old Celeste felt as if the sounds of people talking fell away into silence and the day-lit world was swallowed up in night; there upon the darkened theater stage of the desert floor, she envisioned the early-morning stillness of July 16, 1945, as Richard Feynman, Robert Oppenheimer, and a handful of other observers waited in the bluish pre-dawn stillness, many of them lying down in the otherworldly desolation of the New Mexico desert, expecting an explosion that would shake the mesa beneath them. She imagined the unearthly flash of heat, the searing light illuminating the desert world, and the hallucinatory midnight vision of a darkly blooming rose, with a rolling ball of smoke that slowly ascended, its interior luminous with unfathomable heat, licking the roof of the sky, the vision of a phantom taking its seat upon a spectral throne. Celeste wondered if the rising tendrils of this artificial sun had, perhaps, briefly cast an irradiated glow upon the ruins of the Anasazi dwellings carved into the far-off cliffs of Mesa Verde, the desolation of one century touching the desolation of another. And in 1966, twenty years after the explosion occurred, young Celeste stood at the locus of that ghastly awakening, gazing at the stone monument, a taciturn piece of flotsam from the shipwreck of the world, standing where once had stood the steel tower that held the bomb, the steel armature which had been vaporized in a moment — an apt metaphor for certain conceits of human civilization. In that moment, another memory had sprung unbidden to Celeste's mind: when she was twelve, there had been a bomb drill at her school. Kids had hunched beneath their desks, holding their hands over their heads, rehearsing the action of shielding themselves from the dark promise of atomic energy. That afternoon, after the drill, Fernão had told her the nuclear blast would instantly turn kids into skeletons. "But that's what's going to happen anyways," he said. "That's what time does over seven or eight decades; the bomb just speeds it up." He was in high school, which at the time seemed an age of maturity and wisdom, so she figured he knew.

21.

Celeste stood awhile in quiet thought before the overgrown fireplace, then continued her journey along the meandering path. The roof of the forest seemed to lighten again, growing brighter; here and there clear patches of blue sky could be seen amidst the branches, an electric azure peeking out from behind the chartreuse tracery of leaves. It was as if the woodland had been hushed out of respect for the engulfed cairn of a ruined house, and it had grown merry again now that Celeste had emerged from that shaded gallery.

She came to a meadow where the trees fell away and the forest seemed to open up directly to the sky, an oculus into boundless space. Above her ranged enormous towers of puffy clouds, their edges gilt a blinding white by the sun. A flock of birds wheeled far above, tiny black silhouettes against a creamy white massif of piled cumulonimbus. Suddenly Celeste felt acutely aware that she was standing upon the globe of the earth, and that before her

was a portal into the vastness of the universe —
that behind the cerulean veil lay countless stars in
their ancient arrays, alongside planets, suns, galax-
ies, clouds of interstellar gas and fields of cosmic
dust, and that she herself was on a spinning ball
in the midst of that empyrean realm, upon one
blessed green-and-blue orb amongst myriads of
myriads of other planets. She felt almost dizzy
with the thought, flooded with a sense of awe at
the terrestrial gravity which mercifully bound her
to the earth, like a seat belt keeping her from spinning off into the star-pierced blackness of space.
In that moment, looking up into an immense well
of sky, she fleetingly saw her own fragility in the
grand scheme of things, as if glimpsing the unseen
pillars of creation upon which the earth was borne
perpetually, the perfect point upon which her life
and the life of the planet rode. She felt seized by an
overwhelming sense of gratitude.

The flock of birds disappeared behind a cloud bank,
and Celeste's attention became absorbed in the slow
movement of the inscrutable shapes above, which
gradually expanded and took on new forms as they
traversed wide-open sapphire plains. Watching
the clouds was like observing a ballet enacted with
painfully slow precision, or an ever-shifting series
of sculptures taking on, then subverting, then
discarding one shape after another. There was a
subtle music to the sky, Celeste thought to herself,

and she wondered why she didn't pay more attention to it, to this grand amphitheater which stood perennially open to any who wished to notice.

Celeste walked across the meadow, a great sea of grass trembling and rolling with the breath of the wind, which tickled the back of her neck as it passed by. Reentering the woodland corridor, Celeste smiled as she saw a furtive figure in red darting behind a tree: a fox fleeing her unexpected intrusion.

Here, mantled in the shadows of the forest canopy, Celeste felt as if she were in a kind of womb-like enclosure, a world outside the world; it felt inconceivable that right now, upon the very same earth, wars were being fought, people wept in bitterness, and poverty, sickness, and decay continued their ancient rampage. The intrusions she'd encountered of outer civilization while staying upon the estate — whether via a stray snippet of the evening news she saw while passing by a TV in the common room, or the occasions in which she looked at the newspaper which was delivered to the manor-house every morning — gave Celeste the sensation of watching an immense machine of unfathomable complexity slowly but inexorably lurching out of the control of its ostensible masters, like some Cyclopean engine bucking its mounts and veering toward the observation deck, prompting a sickening sense of imminent doom in those standing and watching from afar.

But out here in the quiet of the wood, those troubles felt very far away, merely the rumor of a storm upon the surface of the sea when seen from the vantage point of the ocean floor, by one safely hidden in soft-lit aquamarine fields of undulating kelp and silent coral castles. Yet Celeste knew that the same disease which gripped the outer world had touched this forest, too, though at this moment, it felt hard to imagine that war or human civilization, or even time itself, could ever touch this sleeping world, could ever infiltrate the twilight silence of these still, tall trees.

22.

Celeste walked on, and time passed. The minutes she spent observing the natural world and passively enjoying what this richly layered landscape evoked within her turned to hours, with still no sign of any diverging path or indication of the way back to the estate. From time to time, she would become aware of the fact that the day was lengthening on, and a sense of panic would sweep over her — a feeling like vertigo, of being lost in a green labyrinth. She would stop in her tracks and look around, trying to ascertain a different route, or alternately she would quicken her pace to a run, in the wild hope that the next turn of the trail might yield answers. But whenever this panic rose within her, she found herself subject to a competing sensation: that of a deep calm which seemed to arise from the very forest itself, as if the trees were exerting a soporific effect. Thus the fear of being lost would crest and fall away, like a gently passing wave, subsumed in a feeling of forgetful contentment. The warmth of the sun, the dappled tapestries of moss and leaf, the soft chattering of birds and tide-like wash of the wind, it all contributed to a sense of well-being, an unreasoning trust that if she simply continued to follow the path, she would eventually find her way back.

So her thoughts drifted lazily, languidly, like a raft in some sargasso sea, bathed in the narcotic haze of afternoon sunlight. Images and moments from childhood arose in her mind, one after the other in webs of tenuous connection, washing up like flotsam borne by the cryptic whims of some internal tide.

It's funny, she thought to herself, the memories that aren't tethered to any specific incidents — the memories that float freely, appearing in fragments, turning up like loose change in a purse. She remembered visiting an aquarium once, at some unspecified point in her childhood, standing before a wall of thick glass, behind which diaphanous clouds of jellyfish swam, suspended in liquid space. She remembered being thirteen and gazing upon the mystifying heraldry delicately etched upon the wings of moths and butterflies; she was sure it meant something, and yearned to know exactly what. She remembered as a teenager strolling along a beach — Santa Barbara, was it?

— on a family vacation, collecting pieces of colored glass rubbed smooth by the sea, and stopping at some point to look at a copse of eucalyptus trees, their naked bark glowing in the electric blue of a Californian twilight. She thought of her Arizonan hometown on late Friday and Saturday afternoons, when the voices of children playing would echo across backyards, bouncing off sheds and houses and fences, off trees and trellises, refracting upwards into the widescreen, technicolor sky, into the lenticular clouds and azure mountain ranges rising in the haze. She remembered the way the wind blew across the coarse tan grassland of the high desert, and the way the horizon would smolder long after the sun had set, so that as a child Celeste would fall asleep looking out her window at the late-night afterglow gradually fading from the sky.

Thoughts like these occupied Celeste as she continued along the woodland path. Unbeknownst to her, she was walking further and further away from her destination.

23.

The sunlight was slanting now, the shadows of trees gradually lengthening as the earth wheeled upon its axis, turning away from the daystar and slowly sliding into night. The sky had turned a deep, gradient sapphire, with the tableaux of clouds colored hues of a rich and piercing gold. It had always seemed to Celeste that there was something particularly poignant about late afternoon sunlight; much of what she remembered from ages ten through twenty seemed to have taken place within that honeyed light, as if those years had been coated in amber. Perhaps it was because after days spent in the interior of a classroom, some of her most potent memories had occurred on weekday afternoons, while waiting to get picked up from school, or playing soccer in a park with friends as the day began to wane, or walking home from the library and crossing autumnal fields.

Glancing at the stately beech and oak and spruce that stood all around, gilded in the waning light,

Celeste thought of the rings that lay hidden within the trunks of those trees — the etched memories of a long history, marking the succession of nights and days, seasons and years, and bearing the residue of ancient storms and icy winters. These rings were the inarticulate memory of the living forest, involuntarily keeping time for the world.

After a while, the night life of the woodland began to appear. A pair of bats wheeled about in crazy circles, silhouetted darkly in the twilight air, and in the distance, Celeste thought she could see dimly phosphorescent lines unevenly arrayed upon the ground. Glowworms, she realized. Growing up, she had always found the idea of bioluminescence — light emitted by life — tantalizing, and one of the highlights of her childhood had been seeing a cloud of fireflies coruscating and pulsing one evening on a camping trip to northern Arizona.

At one point in junior high, Celeste had voraciously devoured library books on the subject of luminous insects, memorizing the names and types of various fireflies, lightning beetles, and railroad-worms, and she'd repeat the name of her favorite bug, the

Pyrophorus nyctophanus — meaning "fire-bearing night-shiner" — under her breath at odd times, like a comforting secret password, a reminder that there were wonderful things in the world. And of all the South American creatures her father had told her and her brother of — the emu-like rheas, the giant anteaters and maned wolves, the oversized armadillos and lithe-backed panthers he had described in an effort to instill in them some of his unwavering love for Brazil — the *Pyrophorini* beetles were those which most captivated Celeste's imagination, with their evocative Latin name and mysterious cold fire. Her father had told her how, upon sultry, humid nights in the Brazilian *cerrado*, in the weeks after the first rains, you could see pinpricks of green fire upon the surface of the great termite mounds that dotted the landscape like sunken monuments from an unknown civilization. One day, she had promised herself, she would see that beetle-light in the tropical savanna it was native to, though that day had not yet come.

Presently, a new phenomenon entered the Black Forest, drifting in with the onset of evening: a thick fog descending from the northern reaches of the wood, languidly enlacing the trees and winding its way around the trunks of oaks and the limbs of aspen, enveloping the world in a cold embrace, holding the world in thrall.

A night bird flew by, flapping wildly in the damp air, piercing the heavy silence like a knife. For no particular reason, a momentary impression came into Celeste's mind, appearing more as a web of tenuously connected visuals than a solid mental picture, but carrying with it a forcefulness that branded itself upon her memory: the vision of a huge cavern within a mountain, containing a hollowed-out realm of moss, stalactites, ice caves, and a sprawling village of lights.

Just as quickly as the impression had appeared, it darted away, like a fox disappearing back into the underbrush. Celeste wondered what subconscious mental process that thought had sprung from, but presently she brought herself back to the task at hand: what to do.

It was getting dark, and while Celeste did not have a particularly strong fear of being alone in the woods at night — she had done quite a bit of hiking over the years, having gone on backpacking trips with her father when she was a teen and spent plenty of time wandering alone in the Arizona wilder-ness — she also realized she was in a particularly strange situation: in a vast forest, in an unfamiliar country, and not having found her way back to the estate for over 24 hours now. Thinking back to the stories her father had told her of his wanderings in the Brazilian backcountry, she recalled that he had on more than one occasion gotten lost and, once evening had fallen, had simply laid down and slept wherever he was. "Better to make your bed on the earth than stumble around in the dark," he would say, eyes twinkling as he feigned the tone of a gnomic proverb. She saw the wisdom of that — and the Black Forest certainly seemed a much safer place to lie down than the South American *sertão;* after all, she hadn't ever heard about deadly snakes or panthers inhabiting the German woodland. Her odds of finding her way back would be much greater in the morning light than in the thick mists of evening.

It was with this in mind that Celeste came to a halt and, finding a spot of even, relatively dry ground, lay down upon it. She was grateful to have worn her poncho, for it was thick enough that it functioned as a kind of blanket-cum-sleeping-bag, which was helpful now that the evening, while not frigid, was growing colder. Interlacing her fingers behind her head, Celeste leaned back and looked up at the silhouetted canopy of interlacing beech branches above her. It was exquisite, she realized, as she traced its pattern-work with her eyes; the beauty of this woven lattice against the dusk-green leaves seemed to grow the more she looked at it. How many corners of the world, she wondered to herself, were filled with similar delights — seemingly mundane details that, when concentrated upon, revealed a hidden splendor that was almost intoxicating?

From somewhere within the gloom of the forest came the dull thud of a plum falling to the ground.

24.

The sun had sunk from view now, and the world was bathed in a lapis-lazuli darkness. From the depths of the fog-clad forest came the muffled sounds of night creatures: the hoots of owls, indistinct scuffling noises, the muted chirp of crickets.

A wave of anxiety again rose within Celeste, a dizzying sense of her own lostness. She closed her eyes and took a deep breath. It was so quiet out here, she thought she could dimly hear the hushed throbbing of blood in her own veins. A flash of memory came to her: the feeling of being twelve and coming in from the backyard, panting and out of breath from running, and her dad coming over and rumpling her hair, then pointing one of his thick, calloused fingers toward her heart. "You feel that?" he said in that pleasantly thick Portuguese accent of his, "Every beat is the gift of life extended, a moment of time given to you by God himself, a moment in which to know him."

Celeste's parents were deeply religious, though they had not always been that way. After the Brazilian *coup d'état* of 1964, Celeste's father and mother realized they might not ever be able to return to the land of their birth, and became politically disillusioned. Around the same time, a new family moved into their neighborhood, and through a series of racially tinged remarks and angry glares, made it clear that they took issue with Celeste's family living on the same block. A heavy cloud seemed to hang over the Nascimento home through the summer of '64, as both her parents wrestled with a profound depression in different ways. Sometime in winter, Celeste's father began attending a Bible study at a coworker's home, and in time, her mother joined him. Slowly, the cloud lifted from their home, and ever since then her parents had been deeply committed to Jesus. She recalled what it was like to lie in bed on Wednesday nights, hearing through her bedroom walls the muffled sound of voices, acoustic guitar, and sometimes a tambourine — the music of her parents' weekly church group. Celeste had found something deeply affecting about the timbre of those earnest voices raised in song; she'd often drift off to sleep listening. Even now, the memory had a comforting effect, and she felt her eyelids drooping as she lay there upon the ground thinking back on those nights.

But Celeste found herself abruptly pulled back from the cusp of sleep, awaking with a start at the sound of a footfall from somewhere close by. Rapidly glancing around her, she saw the misty silhouettes of trees like tall dark poles among the fog; it seemed as if the whole world were swathed in thick blue smoke. Then, off to the east, she saw movement: someone was coming toward her. As the figure drew nearer, the mists seemed to part, allowing her to see an older man wrapped in a dark-gray felt cloak. He was of medium height, with a trim, fit build that felt incongruous with the immense snow-white beard he sported. His black boots glistened with night dew. Celeste realized he was walking straight toward her. She got up and took several steps back.

The man's voice cut through the evening air in German: "Woah, there — I mean you no harm. You're on my property, but I'm not here to scold you. I assume you're lost?" It hadn't occurred to Celeste that she might have strayed onto another estate, and the man's voice, though deep and gritty, sounded earnest and well-meaning.

"I'm sorry, I... I am indeed lost," said Celeste tentatively, feeling once more an acrid sense of panic rising within her. She felt embarrassed and scared, and very much aware of the clumsiness of her American-accented German.

"Don't worry, young lady; I consider you no tres-
passer, but rather my guest. It's late, and if you've
been wandering for some time now — which I take
it that you have — you will no doubt be hungry."

Celeste did not say anything, and was wrestling in
her mind as to whether she should trust this man;
he did seem benign, but she sensed something else:
a certain hiddenness.

"My manor is not far from here. In fact, we're
already upon its northern outskirts. My staff will

be happy to provide you a meal and a warm bed for the night."

"I... don't want to impose," Celeste stammered, still caught in indecision.

"Ah, you've no need to fear me," the man said with a smile, sensing her underlying concern and stretching both his hands out in a gesture of openness. He switched his speech to English: "You have an American accent. Well, not all the Western world has forgotten the Abrahamic virtue of hospitality. You'll find there are still some who consider it an honor to offer shelter to a stranger."

Studying his face, Celeste sensed a courtly air about him; there was indeed an aspect of something hidden about him, yet she perceived now that it was not a covert motive or a secret shame that remained withheld from view, but rather a strangely out-of-time quality about him, as if he were not entirely of the century in which he found himself... He felt like a visitor from a different age. She decided he could be trusted.

"Thank you," she said, "I will certainly take you up."

The man seemed gratified, and bowed benevolently. "My name is Holzfäller — Aldrich Holzfäller

— and my estate lies just a short distance this way." He motioned northward, and began walking confidently through the darkened undergrowth. Celeste followed, half-wondering if she was perhaps still asleep.

25.

Celeste had been unsure what to expect from Holzfäller's estate — whether it would be a well-kept country chateau, or perhaps a dilapidated mansion gone to rot, or possibly even a modest cabin which was an estate in name only. After running through these potential scenarios in her mind, Celeste felt a tantalizing curiosity as they drew closer, a curiosity that intensified when she caught a glimpse of the distant glow of yellow lights burning in the blue-tinted darkness of the sky.

A few moments later, Holzfäller took a right turn, and suddenly they were facing a high hedge of perfectly manicured beech, a sheer wall of solid greenery standing a story high. Holzfäller made his way eastward along the wall, Celeste trailing after him and staring at the wall, which extended as far as she could see in both directions before fading away into the depths of the evening air. After about a minute, Holzfäller halted, and then appeared, from Celeste's vantage point, to step into the hedge itself and vanish.

Drawing closer to where her host had disappeared, Celeste saw that there was a doorway of iron tracery set within the hedge, and Holzfäller stood on the other side of the hedge-wall, courteously holding the door open for her. She nodded her thanks and stepped in, and as she did so, stopped still in her tracks, as the fog seemed to part in order to reveal Holzfäller's estate in its fullness. It simultaneously surpassed and subverted Celeste's expectations.

Past the hedge gate lay a sprawling vista of dilapidated splendor: the image of a grand estate which, though still aglow with opulence, had clearly fallen into a state of mild disrepair. Celeste saw before her acres of assorted rotundas, pools, and arbors — many beautiful and well-preserved, but some appearing worn and tired, littered by broken pieces of marble, or marred by a cracked pillar here or a fallen trellis there; dead leaves floated on the surface of the pools and lay in drifts at the feet of Greco-Roman gazebos — and all around the landscape were tufts of tall grass, which glowed a dull gold in the bluish darkness. There were rows of statuary and paths winding all around, and set within the middle of this Romantic landscape was an immense, four-storied manor of pale marble, rising out of a bed of white gravel which resembled a moat of pebble.

The mansion likewise appeared to have faded from a former state of glory, with tendrils of ivy ascending its walls, the marble marred by areas of discoloring, and tiles fallen from the roof in places — yet still it gave the impression of being a thriving world unto itself, with dozens of tall windows ablaze with light. Patches of mist hovered over the grounds, and thick clouds covered much of the sky, but there were torn openings in a few places, beyond which trembling white stars could be seen within the vault of the firmament. Celeste was stunned.

Holzfäller did not appear to have any desire to awe Celeste with the grandeur of his estate, neither did he apologize for its somewhat disheveled condition. Instead, without affect, he simply motioned for her to come up the main pathway, which led directly to a grand double-doored entrance. "There'll be a warm meal and roaring fire all ready," he assured her amiably. Celeste followed him, somewhat dazed at the aged opulence of her surroundings, as he walked up the leaf-strewn path, which was flanked on either side by stately aspen trees whose leaves glistened in reflected starlight and quivered in a gentle night wind.

Upon reaching the palatial landing, passing two large lion statues that stood on either side of the entrance, Holzfäller rapped on the immense oak doors, the panels of which featured elaborate carvings of rustic scenes, though the forms thereon had softened with age, the long years of use gradually wearing the engravings away.

The doors opened from within, and a middle-aged valet, dressed in the finery of a former age — which fit in with the generally antiquated atmosphere of the place — greeted them in German. "Welcome back, sir. And welcome to you, young lady," he added cordially with a nod toward Celeste.

Holzfäller led the way as they stepped into a well-lit reception area that led onto a great hall, which, like the exterior, evinced a certain crestfallen longing for an earlier grandeur. It was indisputably luxuriant: the corniced walls were hung with tapestries, Persian rugs, and lush paintings depicting muddled dawns over endlessly rolling green hills and tracts of European countryside seen in viridescent splendor; the floor was of polished marble, and the walls were inset with glass display cases, which held a dizzying array of artifacts, taxidermy, bronze figurines, blown glass, and mementoes from all over the globe. Here also were the traces of a slow decay — not an outright dissolution, but a gradual wearing away. The ceiling featured a painted fresco of a golden-blue sky with blustery-looking clouds, but the plaster in a few portions had been chipped away; the floor rugs showed a few thread-bare patches in need of repair, and the large glittering chandelier at the center of the hall, though streaming with brilliant light, betrayed the absence of a few gas bulbs upon its many-armed candelabra.

Celeste took all this in within a moment's glance, and despite noticing the subtle traces of deterioration, her overall feeling was one of awe at the sheer splendor of the place.

Holzfäller took off his felt cloak, hanging it upon a bronze stand by the door, and offered to take Celeste's poncho. She obliged, noticing as she did so that Holzfäller was dressed in a way that seemed to indicate his status as a member of the German nobility — a look that now, in 1972, struck Celeste as utterly ancient. And yet here in this decaying mansion, with a butler dressed in similarly archaic attire, Holzfäller did not feel anachronistic, but elegant and of a piece with the entire estate. If anything, Celeste was the one who seemed out of time, standing there with her blue jeans and weathered Chuck Taylors. Nonetheless, she sensed nothing but welcome from her host.

The valet ushered them into the grand hall, conducting them to a long banquet table of rich, burnished wood. An array of food — various cheeses, cured venison, salted pork, fresh bread, dried fruits, and a large cauldron of hearty-looking soup — lay there before them, and so they sat down to sup.

26.

"You like that piece," Holzfäller said, noticing Celeste gazing thoughtfully at a silver statue of a stag in a display case set within the wall.

"It's quite beautiful, but there's something sad about it, in a way that I can't quite put my finger on," Celeste said quietly.

"Yes," Holzfäller replied, looking curiously at Celeste's expression, as if he detected a note there that he had not expected to find. "The sculptor managed to imbue it with a sense of mourning without veering into the dangers of a turgid anthropomorphism. It feels sad, but sad the way nature is sad. Like the quiet, sad beauty of a meadow in late afternoon."

The deer's stance did indeed look noble but also somehow melancholic, the way taxidermied animals appear simultaneously majestic and tragically out of place when mounted upon a hunter's wall, with something in their glassy eyes betraying the sickly artificiality of their situation.

Celeste looked at the silver stag for a while longer, then resumed her meal. They ate quietly for a time, the grand hall echoing with the soft tinkling of cutlery. It was the kind of place, thought Celeste, that had likely hosted many a banquet over the course of centuries, and she was sure that many dignitaries and men and women of renown had likely sat at this same table. In all likelihood, the place had looked then exactly as it did now, only fresher and filled with life as well as light. Celeste felt a thrill at the sense that the beauties of a bygone age had played out in the very same room, but the thrill was accompanied by a feeling of deep loneliness, for now the hall was occupied by only three figures: herself, the valet, and the master of the house.

"You can feel the history here, I take it," said Holzfäller, as if reading her very thoughts. He smiled wanly and took a draught of wine from a thick goblet of Venetian glass. "This is a venerable estate indeed, having gone back many generations in my family — I inherited it from my father and he from his, and so forth back into the earlier ages of the world. It has seen better times, yes, but I will proudly tell you that I have intentionally let it go to ruin."

The valet, who was standing by a pillar several paces away from the table, at the ready if called for, shifted his stance uncomfortably.

"Yes, let it go to ruin, I said," Holzfäller went on, anticipating Celeste's surprise. "You see, shortly before our beloved Germania" — he spoke the name strangely, as if it filled him with genuine love as well as a simultaneous revulsion — "attempted to destroy itself in its second profane descent into paganism, I became greatly troubled by an awareness of my own family history: this pleasure palace you see before you was built by peasants, 'peasants' at the time being a more genteel word for slaves. My familial wealth is an alloy of that which has been honestly earned and that which has been bought in blood, and so I've attempted to divest myself of the majority of my wealth, leaving me with enough to scrape by, though not enough to maintain this grand lady" — here he indicated the manor itself, gesturing upward with both hands to the high-ceilinged hall — "in the style to which she had become accustomed. But no matter, for I sleep easy at night now." Holzfäller flashed a disarmingly warm, unforced smile, and Celeste believed he genuinely meant what he said, though she suspected there was more to the story. "And now, I wait," he added. "I wait the way the whole world is waiting."

He looked off into the distance now, as if he were seeing through the walls of his manor and out, out into the pitch-black eaves of the forest that lay beyond, out into the darkness of some dripping hollow. Some time passed before he spoke again:

"You know somewhere out there, hidden within the belly of the forest, there is a huge clock face, the biggest I've ever seen. Centuries old, it was mounted on a tall wooden scaffold within a clearing in the forest. The Meadow Tower, locals called it, and people used to go out and picnic by it, and on festival days, entire villages would congregate there, men, women, and children laying out tables and feasting in the shadow of the clock — a potent metaphor, I suppose. But in the years of the First World War, the clock's upkeep was neglected; the tower was forgotten, and the beams of the scaffolding eventually succumbed to decay. The clearing became overgrown, reclaimed by the forest. I came across the old clock once as a boy, by accident, when I got lost on my way to a neighboring village. I was walking through a sea of tall grass and found to my surprise the immense clock face half-buried in the ground, wreathed in moss. I hadn't known what it was at the time — my grandfather later described to me the Meadow Tower's place in the old village festivals — but I did find the scene strangely moving, seeing that mechanism of such fine-tuning and craftsmanship, once surely a source of pride for the inhabitants of the area, now turned over to the elements."

Holzfäller looked at the dark wine in the cup before him.

"It strikes me that the decay which permeates the world, both biologically as well as in the rise and fall of nations and civilizations, is also happening in compressed form within my own life. My body is well along in the process of wearing out. At seventy-three, I am far past the point in life in which the body begins to shudder toward disintegration, like a rollercoaster which has reached its zenith and now prepares to lurch down the crest it once ascended. Yet the promise of renewal will be fulfilled in my body as it will for the cosmos. 'Like a garment they will be changed.'"

Holzfäller turned and looked directly at Celeste with an intensity that, though not malevolent, was off-putting. He had the earnest air of a man telling someone something that he wished someone had told him when he was young. He motioned toward another item in a nearby glass display case — a collection of preserved butterfly chrysalides. "Take a lesson from the larva in its cocoon: the world lies wrapped in a gauze. One day the veil will be ripped away, the midnight hour of which Kierkegaard spoke, when all masks come off."

Celeste listened, but did not say anything.

Holzfäller continued. "I think that, at least in some subterranean way, you sense the truth in what I speak. You can feel it in the earth all around you, and within yourself as well: a great, swelling longing, rising from the basement of the world, an inarticulate hope felt even, I think, by the animals. The promise at which spring is a mere foretelling — a joyful foretelling, yes, but also a portent against everything that is vile and twisted about humankind and its history."

Glancing outside at the pockmarked gray moon peeking between the window curtains, Holzfäller suddenly seemed to become aware of the time, and sat up in his chair.

"Ah now, it's getting late. Time for us all to sleep." With this, he gestured to his valet, who stepped away for a moment and then came back with two lit candles, ready to usher Celeste to bed. Holzfäller rose and thanked her for kindly listening to an old man, then left.

27.

Celeste was led by candlelight down a long hallway, passing a series of ornate doors until finally, the valet stopped before a particular door and opened it. Within lay a spacious room furnished in 19th century style, and dominated by a large, plush-looking bed with four carved posts upholding a red velvet canopy. The valet wished her good evening, and left one of his candles with her, closing the door after him with a click. She could hear his footsteps going back down the corridor, growing softer until they faded from earshot.

Turning back to the bedroom, she briefly shone the candle around the room, finding it clean and well-kept, appearing just as pleasantly arranged as any luxurious European hotel room she might imagine — despite the manor's complete lack of electricity. The decor reminded her of a restrained interpretation of what she imagined an apartment in Versailles would look like: elegant, comfortably appointed, and colored in pinks, creams, whites, and vermillion, replete with wallpaper patterns depicting scenes of rococo aristocrats lounging among overgrown gardens and parks, framed in curling botanicals and twisting vines.

To her surprise, Celeste felt a deep sense of safety in this room, and, quietly delighted by the prospect of a calm night in this plush bed, she was ready to sleep. Since she had no change of clothes on hand, she simply took off her poncho, dropping it to the ground, and crawled under the covers. She blew out the candle, and the yellow glow which had engirdled her disappeared, making visible the subtleties of the darkened room.

The moonlight through the curtains cast coruscating shadows upon the opposite wall, and Celeste found herself studying the folds in the crushed-velvet canopy above the bed. Outside she could hear the wind as it whistled over roof tiles and murmured along walls, skimming along fields and bodies of water, over rivers and through trees, all as it rushed off on some unknowable errand.

The enclosing darkness of this antiquarian-feeling room reminded Celeste of somewhere else she had been: she fumbled drowsily to recall exactly where, dimly recognizing at the same time that she was about to cross the threshold of sleep. Just before she nodded off, she realized what this place, with its time-capsule ambience, felt like to her: the alluring darkness of a Natural History Museum gem hall, with rock crystals and peridotite glowing in an unending artificial night. She'd visited one such museum as a child on one of her family road trips. Though she couldn't recall the city or the year of her visit, she remembered well what stepping inside that hall had felt like — it was like entering a cave deep beneath the earth, a subterranean lair filled with the stone flowers of the mineral kingdom.

28.

Celeste woke up feeling the warmth of the early morning sunlight streaming through the curtains. Sitting up, she found herself enclaved in a crumpled tapestry of sheets; it appeared she'd done a lot of tossing and turning that night, though she'd slept heavily. Yawning, she got up and walked over to the eastward window.

Outside, the mauve crest of a rising dawn was gracefully riding over the back garden — a sprawling topiary landscape laid out symmetrically in a great rectangle whose perimeter was hemmed in by high, evenly spaced trees, and whose center contained a large labyrinth of green hedges, all rimmed with golden light. Celeste almost gasped, the sight was so unexpected and almost comically elaborate.

Having dressed, Celeste stepped out into the hallway. She could hear the distant tinkle of cutlery and movement from somewhere down the hall. She made her way toward it, realizing as she did so that she was quite famished. Walking down the long corridor, past door after door leading into what she assumed were chambers just as lushly furnished as the one she'd spent the night in, Celeste was once more struck by the grandiosity of the place. The curved ceiling above her was painted, a detail she had not noticed the night before, and featured the imagery of a woodland hunt, replete with dogs, stags, hares, and aristocrats on horseback against a background of verdant copses and broad meadows.

The more Celeste studied the style of the painting itself, the more convinced she became that it must have been painted by the same hand as the frescos she was restoring in the Schloss Fernweh lodge — either that, or it was an especially well-studied imitation. Or perhaps, it struck Celeste, perhaps the painting in the lodge was the imitation, and this the original article. In fact, the more she'd seen of this immense mansion, the more she had the sense of being in the Platonic form of a great manor of old, a superannuated image of wealth and opulence...

As she reached the end of the corridor, it turned to reveal not an opening into a larger room as she had expected, but a multiplicity of other passageways forking off in different directions. Though she was somewhat anxious to leave the manor, she felt bemused rather than alarmed at the labyrinthine corridors which presented themselves to her, and she amiably strolled down them, knowing that sooner or later she would have to reach a landing or stairwell leading downstairs. The painting on the ceiling continued in the same style, interrupted from time to time by interludes of gilded molding which framed different segments of the ongoing fresco. The imagery continued in a pastoral vein, a long scrolling tableaux that moved from summer hunting parties and rustic Alemannic villages, to evocative wintry landscapes of bare black trees and snow-capped huts with smoke rising from their chimneys, to profusions of springtime flowers and ivy-clad castles overlooking lakes of mirrored silver.

When Celeste's brother was young, he had been obsessed for a time with digging holes in the backyard, and Celeste's father had delighted in indulging his son's interest. Together he and Fernão would embark upon regular backyard excavations on late afternoons and weekends. Little Celeste would sit on a windowsill and watch them as they filled the yard with holes, and she shared their delight in the process: she sensed along with Fernão an inarticulate thrill of exhilaration at uncovering what lay below the skin of the earth, of seeing the red loam that lay below the sandy top layer, and then the dark, rich soil which lay below that. It was the feeling of getting closer to the root of things. She had sensed this, too, as a teenager, when she began asking her parents questions about how they grew up and began hearing darker stories of their youth: of her father's abusive father, and her mother's ailing mother, of political instability, of the legacy of slavery that haunted Brazil — a slavery which had only been banished less than a generation before her parents' birth. As she heard those stories, Celeste began to see how there were layers upon layers of a family's — and a country's — history, and how this history had left its mark upon who her parents were now.

She felt something of that same sensation now, of getting under the surface to a deeper layer of reality. This manor felt somehow like the deeper, truer manor, the archetype, of which the Schloss Fernweh estate was a pale reflection.

There was also a weird pervasive sadness here. A question arose in her mind: *who built this place?* and the guessed-at rejoinder followed: *the local peasants.* How strange, these palaces of culture and glittering things — not just here, but in so many places and societies all over the world — which attempt to embody heights of sublime aspiration and beauty, and yet are usually built upon the backs of the poor and bedraggled. Smuggled within these bright edifices of glimmering architecture is the implicit darkness of the human heart, of a corruption that lingers no matter how desperately it yearns for purity.

Presently, Celeste reached the end of a passageway and, turning, emerged into a large landing upholstered in rich red velvet, at the center of which lay the top of a staircase which descended to the main level. A valet, not the one Celeste had seen last night, but a fresh one with an exceptionally crisp-looking mustache, was standing beside the stairs, apparently waiting for her.

"Good morning. The master is out already, but before leaving, he took care to ensure that a fine breakfast would be waiting for you when you awoke. Just downstairs, if you will," he said, motioning down the stairway.

Celeste thanked him and started to head down, but then turned back with a question: "Will he be gone long? I'd like to thank him for his hospitality before I leave."

"He'll likely be gone a long while, at least until late afternoon, I'd say. He's out hunting with his falcons."

"Out hunting with his falcons," Celeste repeated. "Got it." She thanked the valet and bounced down the stairs. "Falconry," she thought to herself, smiling inwardly, "It doesn't get much more Old World than that."

29.

Breakfast took place in the same grand hall as dinner. Celeste sat at the same table as last night, but on a different side, which gave her an entirely different view to contemplate as she ate. The meal itself was delightful, comprising an array of fruit from the local orchard along with biscuits, honey, and cream.

Upon the wall before her hung gold-frame oil paintings portraying an assortment of aristocratic-looking men, women, and children, whom she presumed to be Holzfäller's ancestors, their visages from various time periods all brought together in one space to gaze down upon the living as they ate. One portrait in particular stuck out to her: that of a young man, likely not even seventeen, but possibly older, perhaps even the age Celeste was now. He was garbed in the trappings of old nobility — a fur-lined cloak over a waistcoat and breeches — and stood poised upon a high hill; in the background lay his ancestral home, the very mansion in which

Celeste now sat. The young man's eyes held a look of pride, verging on haughtiness, yet something in his expression also betrayed a hidden insecurity, the look of someone who did not yet quite know his way in the world, even as he stood upon the brink of a vast inheritance. The hardness in his eyes came across as a front, as a stratagem for covering up something soft and vulnerable within him, a tenderness that was slowly calcifying with age.

She looked at the portrait and saw not the pride and power of wealth, but the sadness of a frail creature who thought he could preserve himself from the limits of his own creatureliness. She imagined this young man years later, upon his deathbed, swathed in crumpled mountains of blankets, lying there, unable to rise, with the pretensions of godlike autonomy stripped away by the ravages of time. She looked at this poor young ruler and felt pity for him.

Once breakfast was finished, Celeste rose from the table and, finding the valet standing in the reception area, she asked if he might give her directions to walk back to Schloss Fernweh.

The valet smiled and emphatically shook his head no. "You needn't walk, young lady. Master Holzfäller gave instructions that his carriage is to be at your disposal. Come, look just outside — it's already waiting."

30.

Stepping outside, Celeste was delighted to see that, indeed, a closed carriage led by two dappled-gray horses was waiting upon the gravel by the main entrance, looking for all the world like an illustration from an old storybook. The door of the carriage was open, and a coachman stood at the ready. Turning to the valet, Celeste thanked him and asked him to pass along her sincere gratitude to Holzfäller. The valet smiled and bade her safe travels.

The coachman helped Celeste up into the coach, took his seat at the front of the carriage, and cracked the reins. The horse took off at a trot, and so they were borne away toward the woods. They exited through a large entranceway within the hedge, a different one from that which Celeste had entered through last night, and she craned her head to look at the black iron archway as they passed beneath it; its faux-botanical metalwork was entwined with real vines of living ivy that were gradually creeping upon it. Leaving the estate grounds, the gravel beneath the wheels gave way to a road of tightly packed dirt, and the clacking sound of the horse's hooves softened. Ahead, the road curved away and headed into the woodland.

Just before the carriage plunged into the shadows of the forest canopy, Celeste turned back and caught a glimpse of the Holzfäller estate. Something in her told her she would never see it again, and so she tried to drink in every last drop of that vista, of the leaf-strewn grounds and dilapidated manor shining in the morning sun, before it was swallowed up from view by the passing foliage. She turned back and sat quietly within the carriage. The interior of the coach was colored in a rich emerald velvet with golden-yellow accents, and it was quite comfortable to ride in, though Celeste could detect a faint scent of mildew. She wondered if she had ever actually ridden in a carriage before, and remembered that she had once as a girl at one of the Old West festivals that were occasionally held in small towns in the Southwest. That carriage, though, felt like a simulation of the cowboy era, while this felt like an actual piece of the past, bearing her away from a bygone age and onward toward the present.

The ride was about two hours long, and mostly without incident. Celeste gazed out the window at the green-and-gold rush of trees passing by the window, enjoying the mottled tapestry of light and dark, and the way the sunlight cast a delicate tracery of ever-shifting shadows upon the plush velvet seats of the carriage. At one point, the forest wall to her left opened up, revealing a small river which ran alongside the road for a time. Its brownish-yellow surface was translucent enough to yield a dim glimpse of a sunless inner world of mossy stones and shaggy vegetation, and Celeste wondered if this was the same river she had encountered upon one of her earlier walks. The muddy color of the water struck Celeste as vaguely tropical in appearance, and she could imagine this slender tributary winding its way through some unknown southern continent of humid lagoons and hazy promontories, passing under the shadows of palm fronds and immense ferns.

In time, the road turned away from the river, and the water was lost from sight, disappearing once more into the depths of the verdant woods. Gradually, the corridor in which they rode narrowed considerably, the walls of the forest seeming to close in upon it, and at a turn of the road, one of the back wheels suddenly bucked, sliding off the road and slipping just over the lip of a steep embankment to the left. Feeling the jolt, Celeste braced herself instinctively, and for a horrible moment, it felt as if the horses were stumbling and the carriage was drifting leftward and in danger of tipping. Glancing out the window, Celeste saw that the embankment led down to a lush gully blanketed in dark-green ivy; it was beautiful, and almost seemed to beckon Celeste downwards, as if it were waiting to welcome the coach into its viridian embrace. Thankfully, the horses seemed to recover, and as they surged forward, the carriage regained traction; the wayward wheel was pulled back from the brink, and the moment passed. Celeste let out a sigh, and thought how curious it was that a part of her had somehow wanted to tumble into the gully.

The only other incident of note upon Celeste's journey was that at one point, she saw, far off, a distant path through the trees. "Probably the path I was wandering on yesterday," she thought, and then to her surprise she saw a familiar figure upon it: that of Anise, walking along with her head tilted back, basking in the shafts of sunlight that fell from the thatched canopy of trees. As if sensing Celeste's gaze, Anise looked up and caught sight of the carriage; raising her hand, she waved and smiled, a smile suffused with the same kind of sadness and reserve that Celeste had sensed beneath the surface of their past conversations. Celeste raised her hand in greeting, and smiled gently; a moment later, Anise and the path had disappeared from view, blocked by a particularly dense copse of oak. Celeste felt in that moment as if a chapter in her life were drawing to a close, and her time in the forest was approaching an end.

31.

Eventually, the carriage emerged from the forest into a broad meadow, following the road up a high hill until it joined a broad avenue. To Celeste's surprise, she recognized it as the aspen-lined avenue which led to Schloss Fernweh; they were approaching the road from the direction opposite of what she'd expected. She realized how thoroughly lost she had been, but was grateful to see the familiar outline of the Fernweh manor-house rising against the horizon, like the face of an old friend. Above it the sky shone a brilliant blue, with white puffs of clouds hovering high in the distance.

As the carriage pulled up to the estate's entrance gates, Celeste asked the coachman if he could let her off here. The coachman obliged, bringing the horses to a halt, then hopping down to open the door for Celeste. She thanked him profusely, and he simply bowed courteously.

Walking alone up the long driveway to the main

complex of buildings, Celeste hoped she wouldn't encounter anyone on the way up to her room, for she dreaded the inevitable conversation explaining how she, the wide-eyed American girl, had gotten lost for three days in the forest.

As it turned out, the gardener did happen to catch her by the entrance. "Had a good adventure, did you?" he said, but his manner was kind. Celeste had forgotten that Anise's husband was friends with the gardener, and it struck her that news might travel through the forest, betwixt the various estates and villages, quicker than she might have guessed.

"Was expecting you back yesterday, though," the gardener added, and Celeste explained that she had spent the night at the Holzfäller estate. The gardener seemed surprised, and was keen to ask her several questions about what the estate was like and what sort of man Holzfäller was.

"Have you ever been to Holzfäller's manor?" Celeste asked.

The gardener shook his head, smiling: "I've seen it from afar plenty of times, and when I was younger I used to go prowling about the gardens, exploring. But I've never actually been inside, though I've heard some descriptions from those who have."

"Holzfäller seemed an extremely hospitable man to me," Celeste observed. "I bet he would let you take a look around if you'd only ask."

"Maybe he would at that," the gardener said, thoughtfully. "Perhaps one day I'll go get lost myself," he added, with mirth in his eyes.

Celeste smiled, then excused herself to her room. The rest of the day was calm, and she found that most everyone else on the estate had apparently felt no reason to be concerned about her absence — all of which came as quite a relief to her.

32.

Days passed. Celeste's work continued apace in the mornings, and while she still took walks around the estate in the afternoons, she kept her forest wanderings to a minimum; the thought of getting lost again felt a little too silly to risk. She didn't talk much with anyone, and she hadn't seen Peter in some time; apparently he was off handling business at another property. Celeste simply fell into the quiet rhythms of the estate, read some books, and spent long evenings staring out at the wind gently rippling through the trees upon the woodland's edge, which set her thinking about all that lay in the tantalizing darkness of the forest interior: the crumbling mansion, the overgrown orangerie, the birds and moss, foxes and owls, and the unseen northern fence.

Soon enough, Celeste finished her restoration work on the final fresco, and thus her contract came to an end. She hadn't set an end-date when originally booking her trip to Germany, so she called a local travel agency and got a flight from Stuttgart back to America. So it was that Celeste awoke one bright Wednesday morning, and got up knowing that this was in fact her last day on the estate.

She spent most of that day wandering around the grounds, simply drinking in the atmosphere of the place, knowing she would likely never return. It is strange to spend a specific period of time in a place one has no formal connection to beyond a particular visit, to live among a particular group of people one would otherwise have no contact with, and to do so in the knowledge that years from now, one would likely look back at this season as if it were enclosed within a snow globe, the memories formed here holding a particular potency by virtue of being so disconnected from the rest of one's life.

So Celeste ambled around the edges of the Black Forest, and ate lunch by the poolside, and spent a few hours perusing the manor-house library, with its high bookshelves, some of which were punctuated by marble busts of various German aesthetic luminaries from the past, almost all of whom she didn't recognize. She scanned the spines of the dizzying array of books there, some of which were centuries old and some of which were fairly contemporary.

 She pulled out one rather venerable-looking book entitled *Fairy Tales from the Swabian Circle*, and sat down on a comfortably padded sofa which was flanked on either side by suspended globes — one a topographic map of the earth, the other of the moon. Casually leafing through the book, Celeste admired the faded illustrations in watercolor and woodcut; the book must have been at least a hundred years old. Her eyes fell upon a page featuring the image of a high stone promontory with a small opening in its side, on the threshold of which stood a little figure gazing wistfully out. The accompanying German text read:

> *There is a certain cave high up in a certain mountain, facing east, overlooking a great valley, and on clear days, you can catch a silver glint of the far-off sea. A penniless hermit lives in the recesses of the cave. Every morning he awakes in the pre-dawn stillness and takes his seat upon the stone lip of the cavern, watching as the thick gloom of the valley gradually lightens, turning*

rose-red as it is struck by the first tendrils of the rising sun.

The hermit looks on as the pink mists of the valley rise and dissipate in the morning air, and says to himself: 'All the coruscating colors of the rainbow, the entire spectrum of visible light this world has to offer, can be seen here, from my viewing platform within the womb of the dawn. How rich am I!'

That was all there was to the story; it felt so different from the fairy tales Celeste had heard as a child, distinguished not only by its brevity but also by its strangeness. It felt strange the way life felt strange, the way there wasn't necessarily a clear climax to the events recounted, but the experience felt nonetheless full of depth of meaning, hinting at a shimmering richness lying beneath the surface. In that moment, Celeste recalled the opaque surface of the Pacific Ocean when she had gazed out upon it from a Big Sur cliff during her college trip — those silver waters had felt like a huge, rippling fabric lain atop a world of inexhaustible wonder, teeming with abundant life beneath a sealed dome.

33.

That night before dinner, Celeste packed her belongings into a large brown suitcase her parents had given her shortly before her trip to Europe. After filling it with everything she'd brought except what she'd need that night, she sat down on the bed and gazed around the room. The floral wallpaper was illuminated with a golden light — the curtains were arranged just so, and the sunset was glowing through them, casting the vague shadow-shapes of trees and the dark bar of the window frame upon the muslin surface, which rustled faintly in the gentle evening breeze.

The dinner bell rung downstairs, and Celeste rose and went down to the dining hall. Most of the estate staff were present; several of them knew it was Celeste's final evening with them and so they wished her well.

As they all sat around the long tables, the gardener began telling folk tales which had been passed around Black Forest villages for centuries. Soon enough the gardener had the full attention of everyone present, for he was a captivating narrator. He clearly relished the audience, as he regaled them with stories of strange happenings, anecdotes of wondrous golden birds and various trickster figures, all adorned and embroidered with amusing asides and verbal footnotes, as well as some particular German phrases Celeste didn't know. Celeste was surprised by his eloquence and breadth of knowledge, by the poetry of his cadence, and at one point a woman sitting near her, noting her rapt attention, leaned over and whispered, "My older sister went to secondary school with him; she said he did very well in school, and the teachers encouraged him to study literature in university, but he wanted nothing of it. Still, he reads every book he can get his hands on, and he's the finest storyteller I've ever heard."

One story in particular that the gardener told, one he said had actually happened to him, struck Celeste as feeling weirdly familiar, as if it bore the texture of one of her own dreams. While she later forgot many of the details, the contours of the story remained lodged in her memory years afterward:

"When I was a young man, I spent much time hiking in the great Jura Mountains — the Swabian alps, as we say." He motioned vaguely eastwards. "It was a land of inexpressible beauty. Hiking those gently rolling hills, I took in many sights: fields of rippling golden grass; towering hilltop castles, the mountain strongholds of old; nameless streams burbling happily through earthen folds; profusions of juniper in bloom, spicing the air with their fragrance; sheep grazing in a late afternoon haze; vales and moorlands gently sleeping in the twilight. I remember sitting for hours upon the high brow of a mountain one evening, silently watching a glistening sliver of the Danube in moonlight."

Here the gardener fell silent for a moment, looking off in the distance, as if briefly reliving what it felt like to be young. The moment passed and he resumed: "Now the mountains of Jura are filled with the fossils of creatures long gone: cave bears, giant deer, mammoths, wild horses — along with carved ivory figurines and etchings from the past. Within the alps' limestone bowels, there too lie skeletal remnants of the Roman road that once wound through there, the interred remains of a bygone empire. And the alps are honeycombed with caves — dripstone caverns wending their way through the pitch-black interior of the earth. These days the cave locations are mostly all mapped out and their entrances either closed off or made into tourist attractions. But back when I was young, you might easily stumble across a gaping, darkened hole in some obscure nook or mountain fold and looking in, you'd find yourself peering into the depths of a great cavern.

"One day I came across one such cave mouth, barely visible behind a profusion of bramble bushes. I furtively tossed a stone in, trying to ascertain if there was anything living in there, or if perhaps there might be a pool of brackish water waiting for me to fall into it. There came back an echo of stone clattering against stone, and it seemed to me that it sounded as if the cave went quite a ways back. I took out a flashlight from my rucksack and, flicking it on, cautiously made my way into the hole."

34.

"The tunnel was dry, and went quite a ways back. Apart from the presence of a few scraggly shrubs eking out an existence in the near-perfect darkness, there were no signs of life. The passage continued on, deeper and deeper, gently sloping down, and I sensed that I was stepping down a stairway into the secret sunken places of the earth. Gradually, I became aware of a sound, at first imperceptible but slowly growing in strength and clarity. It was the sound of rushing water. I continued on, as the atmosphere became moist and the walls wet. The notion of discovering a cave river or underground lake sent a thrill through me.

"After a while I reached a point where the tunnel broadened out into a large chamber, which reverberated with the sound of gurgling water. I flashed my electric torch around. A waterway lay at the far end of the chamber, its black liquid splashing as it rushed along a dark channel. I almost jumped when I saw that lying within those waters was a wooden canoe, tethered to the side of the canal. Drawing closer, I observed it to be in good shape; there were no signs of decay, and no evidence of moss growing inside, which made me think it must have been recently used. Two carved oars had been placed inside, and the vessel was tied to a metal post on the cave floor by means of a new-looking leather strap.

"Shining my light along the waterway, I saw that the subterranean river emerged from a wall of rock and flowed at a subtle incline downwards, running the length of the cavern and disappearing through a tunnel within the sheer wall of limestone upon the opposite end of the chamber. Peering at that tunnel, I became convinced it was manmade; while not geometrically perfect, its edges were straight enough that it couldn't have been the result of any natural erosion process.

"At my age now, I would not have done what I did then. But I was young, with no family to consider should something happen to me, and little fear. So after examining the canoe thoroughly, I decided to see where the waterway might lead: I got into the vessel, tied my flashlight to the bow so that it pointed straight ahead, and untied the mooring. As the current slowly took the canoe, I grabbed one of the oars, readying myself in case I needed to stop the vessel from hitting a wall. My initial plan was merely to see what lay a few meters beyond the passage in the wall.

"As the canoe picked up speed, I found the feeling exhilarating. The rock tunnel was large enough that I did not need to duck down as I entered it, and within it lay a long passageway extending as far as my flashlight's beam could carry. The air within the tunnel was cool, and smelled vaguely of bromide. The water that occasionally splashed upon me was ice-cold, and I found it invigorating, like a draught of cold beer on a hot day. I initially kept my oar poised to jab against any low incoming walls or stonework, to prevent myself from being knocked off the canoe, but as I was continually borne along, my sense of vigilance gradually decreased. The passage, while carved out ruggedly and unevenly, was clearly the result of significant excavation work; I was increasingly convinced the watercourse had been made for a mining operation.

"Minutes passed, and it seemed as if the tunnel took a few gentle twists and turns, with the canoe occasionally bumping against one of the damp gray-green walls, but my ride remained relatively smooth and sedate. I'm not sure how much time passed, but I began to wonder how deep I had descended. A sudden thought struck me — lacerated me, I might say — that this chute might perhaps termi-nate in a waterfall over some abysmal precipice, or might leave me washed up upon some subterranean shore, fathoms below the surface of the earth with no means of getting back to the world above. I pictured myself expiring in some Cyclopean hall of enormous quartz deposits, which would reflect back the failing light of my electric torch in a glittering coruscation — but such beauty would provide no means of escape, only an unusually picturesque tomb."

35.

"Happily, as you may guess by my sitting here before you, those fears proved unfounded. In time, the tunnel opened up into an enormous chamber, one which was, to my surprise, dimly lit by a kind of blue phosphorescence. Looking all around me, I saw that I had entered a circular cavern whose rounded ceiling stretched a good seven stories above me. The waterway I was traveling ran straight through the middle of the space, and upon all sides of the room reared huge formations of flowstone, spiraling up in towering columns and weirdly evocative shapes, in dreamlike structures of free-floating abstraction which resembled liquids more than they did solids, but which I knew nevertheless to be made of heavy and immovable rock. Alongside rose immense shafts of dark tourmaline, sprouting like geometric flowers from the ground. The ceiling was a tapestry of ornate stonework, with twisting projections and draperies and frost-like stalactites, gliding like waterfalls frozen in mid-fall, interspersed with great blooms of varicolored crystals.

"Being in that room felt both like being on the moon and being under the sea. I couldn't help but laugh in mixed joy and shock, and my laughter sounded like tinkling glass, dully reverberating in that vast and sunless space.

"The river-current slowed as I entered this cavern, and looking ahead, I could see that the waterway broadened out toward the far end of the chamber, ending in a large pool. Several other canoes of similar make could be seen clustered together there, vacant and bobbing slightly with the current. As I drew near to the pool, I used my paddle to draw close to the embankment; I got up and stepped out of the boat, letting it gradually drift away to the far side of the holding pool. Looking down at my feet, I saw the floor was covered with white orbs of various sizes — cave pearls. I had encountered these before when spelunking with friends. They were like strange mineral fruit. I leaned down and pocketed some, and then walked around, gawking at that mysterious underground plaza.

"The chamber itself appeared to be formed by the inscrutable processes of geology — sculpted by processes of erosion and accretion and upheaval. There are, I suppose, a great many such cavities within the earth, like air bubbles in dough, of which only a few are known to humanity. Evidently someone had somehow found this enormous hall and carved out the winding waterway that led to it; it must have been an undertaking of considerable time and cost. And to what end? Was it some sort of viewing platform, like a gallery for mineral artifacts or an observation deck for looking upon the lower world? I paid particular attention to the dull phosphorescent glow which lit the entire space; it seemed as if there were light sources of some kind placed at strategic points within the walls and ceiling. I could see no source of electricity, and the light was bluish and dim in a way I couldn't quite figure; perhaps it was a growth of luminescent fungi — like the foxfire you find sometimes in rotting stumps in the woods — or something else, I do not know.

"In any case, after wandering around for some time, wondering who in the world built this place and for what purpose, I saw something which I hoped might yield an answer: off in a corner, there was a circular stone hut — almost like a dovecote — which I hadn't noticed at first (it was fairly dim in there, mind you). I made my way over and found it to be made of rocks of various sizes, with an inlaid stone door. The door was closed, but there was no lock, and the whole building radiated heat.

"Dragging the door open — it was quite thick and heavy — I felt a blast of heat and, stepping inside, I began perspiring almost immediately. I found myself in an almost-unbearably hot and stuffy room, at the edges of which were two plain stone benches. In the center of this hut was a bright light coming from a round opening, like a well shaft, in the floor. Taking a few steps forward, I found the sensation of heat increased exponentially, and I couldn't bear getting any closer; I was beginning to feel dizzy. Everything in me wanted to get out of there, to run out into the solace of the cool cavern air, but at this point my curiosity was stronger than my urge to flee.

"Leaning forward, I looked into the bright opening and managed to make out a symmetrical, circular shaft from which a red-and-gold glow emanated. It was blinding, in the intensity of both light and heat, and it seemed as if its interior were dancing and churning, like the bubbling of a cauldron. It dawned upon me that I was looking down a borehole into the innards of the world itself: the fiery glow was coming from the earth's white-hot mantle, and this stone hut functioned as a geological observatory.

"At this point, I couldn't bear to be in there any longer, and abruptly turned and left. After heaving the stone door to a close behind me, I fell down to the ground, exhausted. I must have laid there for a half-hour, breathing heavily, before the dizziness passed and I was able to get up."

At this point in the narrative, the gardener paused for dramatic emphasis, and one of the listeners in the dining room — an older woman named Ana who was head of the kitchen staff — piped up: "So what was that place?"

The gardener shrugged. "I don't know. I never saw anybody in there and, after I got out, I asked around local villages and nobody seemed to know what I was talking about. In years since, I've even asked the few scientists I've come in contact with — I do not necessarily come in contact with many scientists in my profession, mind you," he added with a smile, "but I've asked the few scientists I have met about observatories to study the fiery parts of the earth, and they say it simply can't be done, at least not yet. They said we can't get any of our drilling instruments down that far. So I don't know what that place was."

He fell silent for a moment. His audience was still rapt, for he truly was a masterful storyteller. After a time, a young man, one of the assistant groundskeepers, asked: "How'd you get out?"

"Well, I realized the canoe was useless to me, since I couldn't see any way to go upstream, but I figured whoever used this place must have some way out, so I went along the cavern's rounded wall inch by inch, until finally I found, scarcely visible unless you were right in front of it, a slender staircase carved out of the limestone. Up, up, up it went in a spiraling helix. Ascending it, there were a few times I had to pause and catch my breath, but eventually it led out through a cave mouth on the other side of the hill that I had entered, near a copse of pine trees. The sun was on the verge of the horizon, it was a beautiful, warm summer evening, and I was famished, so I found a village pub as quickly as I could."

36.

Having completed his story, the gardener proceeded to reminisce about his experiences as a young man wandering about Germany. Gradually his monologue turned from anecdotes of his youth into a gentle denunciation of city folk:

"Why do they build such tall cities, higher and higher? I suspect it is because, somewhere inside themselves, they are trying to bury something. We desire to surround ourselves with what our own hands have made so that we may avoid facing the reality of our dependence, our contingency upon the earth. People loathe reminders of their creatureliness; that is why so many of us hate going to the doctor, is it not? We do not like to be told that we aren't in control."

The audience grew restless, and the gardener decided it was time to retire for the night. He rose and put on a battered cap he produced from his pocket. "Well, I must be getting on; tomorrow morning, work begins on repairing a big breach in the northern fence," he said.

On his way out, he came over and bade Celeste farewell, taking both her hands in his and wishing her safe travels. Afterwards, Celeste lingered for a while by the table, and eventually decided to go out for some evening air.

Outside, the upper half of the sky was a deep ultramarine hue that gradually lightened in shade as it came down to meet the horizon, which was still luminous with the fading glow of the now-departed sun. Pinpricks of light were beginning to sparkle in the endless depths of the sky.

Celeste decided to see the paintings in the hunting lodge one last time — it was, she realized, perhaps the last time she would ever see them. Walking over to the lodge, crossing the neatly cut grass, she thought of Holzfäller's dilapidated estate off somewhere in the depths of the Black Forest — the archetype of which this estate, Schloss Fernweh, seemed to be a modest, but thriving, reflection. Or perhaps Holzfäller's estate was a murky, dreamlike inversion of the living microcosm of Schloss Fernweh. In any case, the Holzfäller manor now seemed far away, ensconced within a fertile forest realm that felt centuries removed from the contemporary world.

Presently Celeste reached the hunting lodge, and found the door ajar. Glancing in, she saw Peter sitting there before the roaring hearth, quietly gazing at the fire. Becoming aware of her presence, he looked up and smiled, beckoning her in with a friendly wave.

37.

They both sat in plush, high-backed armchairs that had been fashioned a century before, and their faces glowed in the undulating flicker of the fire. The scene would seem to lend itself to a vaguely romantic, intimate air, but Peter had a way of assuming the friendly, open manner of a brother so that Celeste felt perfectly comfortable and welcome, without any sense that Peter had hidden designs for their time.

"So," Peter said with a nod of his head, eyes glistening in the firelight, "what did you think of the Black Forest, after spending three days lost within it? Did you feel like the protagonist of a folk tale?" Celeste hadn't realized that the story of her travails into the woods had been widely circulated among the staff, but then again, it came as no great surprise — the story of the wide-eyed young American getting lost on a stroll and reappearing days later would have been a story too delightful not to tell. By now, she ruefully imagined, her misadventure was being recounted within the rustic taverns of distant villages.

Celeste thought about Peter's question for a moment, then answered in a roundabout way. She told him about the western edge of her hometown, where there was a long stretch of road that ran north-south and was flanked on either side by large cedar trees which towered with patrician gravity: *Cedrus deodara*, originally indigenous to the Himalayas. The street was known as Christmas Tree Lane, for in a tradition since the early years of the 20th century, residents of the town would walk the road during the Christmas season, looking up at shivering stars framed by a canopy of pitch-black boughs. In time a tradition developed around the trees, and each December volunteers would festoon strings of lights upon the branches, making glowing garlands to illuminate the quiet homes and asphalt street below, in contrast to the darkness of the rolling hills beyond.

"As a little girl, looking up into the eaves of those trees," said Celeste, "I felt like I was looking into an entirely different planet, a world of rich greens and cool shadows, scented with aromatic sap and fragrant needles, offering a verdant place of shade in contrast to the relative barrenness of the surrounding desert. It felt then to me like a hint, a foretaste, of what a vast woodland might be like.

Spending time in the Black Forest, to me, was like finally entering into the world I had sensed a hint of in the shade of those boughs."

Peter smiled at this, and they were both silent for a while. The room was filled with the sound of the fire, punctuated by occasional pops as tiny pockets of water and sap secreted within the logs turned to steam and exploded.

The conversation moved on. Celeste asked Peter who owned the Fernweh Estate, and he told her about the family he worked for — the Jägers — and the way in which he shuttled between their various estates, overseeing the never-ending tasks of keeping up the grounds, accommodating guests and visitors, and ensuring the various factions of the family were all satisfied.

He spoke of the madness of the wealthy, and how his work put him in a position to observe how the members of the family had embarked upon varied individual pursuits in their collective search for an elusive fulfillment. "An excess of money," he observed, without bitterness but rather a sense of pity, "seems to act as a kind of neurotoxin." He told her of his clients' strange extravagances: a banquet which had as its centerpiece a baked seven-foot-long oarfish presented on a bed of edible floral arrangements; a nearby estate with an on-site milliner and tailor in order to keep its bachelor owner continuously bedecked in sartorial splendor; the exorbitant amounts of capital poured into keeping up manors which were occupied a scant few weeks of the year, at most.

It was, Peter had to admit, not always the most satisfying of employments, but he viewed his primary task not as catering to the wealthy heirs, but as providing fair, stable, and pleasant employment to the various employees of the estates — the gardeners, maids, caretakers, attendants, kitchen staff. This, he said, was what made his job enjoyable, along with the actual beauty of the estates themselves.

38.

"So tell me," Peter said, having grown tired of speaking about himself, "are you going to go back to America and become a famous painter?"

Celeste laughed uneasily, bashfully. She had heard many variations of this question from friends and acquaintances since she'd enrolled in art school, and she was never quite sure how to respond. "I do not know what I shall do," she said plainly. "I like painting, but I think... I think I prefer restoration work. I like the feeling of bringing someone else's work back to its original fullness. It feels like... touching a bit of the past. There's a sensation of continuity, of history."

"We're grateful for what you've done here," Peter responded simply, gesturing upwards at the paintings which surrounded them, dimly illumined by the orange flames.

"One thing I am curious about: does anyone know

who actually painted these images?" asked Celeste. "I saw some similar frescos at the Holzfäller estate which looked as if they were by the same person. In all my preparation for this job, I couldn't seem to find any information on the original painter. I studied the painting styles of the time, of course, and works like these are usually anonymous. But I can't help but wonder who it was. Having spent so much time poring over every brushstroke, one begins to feel a somewhat intimate knowledge and connection with the original artist."

Peter shifted in his chair, his eyes sparkling in the dark-golden light. "As a matter of fact, I'd meant to tell you: after we spoke the other month about what you loved about painting, I did some digging. I know a historian in the area who has some connections to the Jäger family, and he told me that though he didn't know definitively, he had a hunch that these paintings were by a man alluded to in regional lore as *Der Wanderer*, who passed through this part of the Black Forest in the early-18th century. There are scraps of village histories which suggest that he was not necessarily a welcome figure, being rumored to be of Moorish or Abyssinian blood — which could really mean anything, those terms being shorthand for any number of non-European countries — but his talents as a painter were apparently universally recognized. Members of the local nobility sought out his skills for the ornamentation of their residences, and it seems it became something of a local fad to have his work enlivening one's walls. That's pretty much all that's known of him: he came through, painted some lovely frescoes, and eventually traveled on along his way."

"Thank you," Celeste said softly, staring thoughtfully at the paintings in the dying light of the fire. She thought of the nameless man who had painted them — the sort of life he must have led, traveling through that very same Black Forest that she had traveled, likely seeing some of the very same trees she had seen, but in their youth. She thought of the loneliness he must have felt, and wondered what he had thought about while applying the very brushwork she had painstakingly traced over, line for line and stroke for stroke. She felt gratitude for now knowing at least a fragment about his life; at least now he was, in some sense, not entirely anonymous.

"And now, I think, I must away to bed," Peter announced, standing up. The fire had sunk down to a few glowing embers. Celeste yawned; she too was ready for sleep. Peter busied himself with closing the fireplace grate.

They emerged into the cobalt darkness of evening, their shadows crisply outlined upon the marble walkway in the brightness of the full moon. The entire world had taken on a sapphire tint; it reminded Celeste of the way Hollywood films usually depicted nighttime by filming in daytime with a heavy blue filter, which lent the proceedings a dreamy quality. In France, they called this effect *la nuit Américaine:* American night.

Celeste and Peter said their goodbyes, and Peter shook her hand warmly. As she made her way back to her room, she heard the flapping of feathered wings overhead and, turning on her heel, caught sight of a white barn owl gliding toward the forest, its black eyes sparkling within a circular white face, its underbelly and pinions shining luminous in the moonlight. Celeste watched as it disappeared into the gloom of the woodland canopy.

She headed off to bed and that night she dreamt of a long, jet-black train chugging its way up a serpentine mountain railway. The train and landscape were bathed in a dense fog, so that the train itself appeared to be winding its way through a dim tunnel of thick mist, which pressed in upon the droplet-studded glass of the passenger windows. At first Celeste seemed to be watching the train from afar, but then, following the logic of a dream — which rarely seems strange to the dreamer — she found herself inside the train, looking out one of those glass windows, gazing out into a world of formless, silvery gray.

39.

Celeste awoke softly, and as the haze of slumber gradually lifted from her mind, she recalled a moment from one of her childhood road trips. She and her family had stopped in Reno for an early dinner at a restaurant adjoining a casino, and while they were eating, an immense fog had descended upon the entire city, cloaking everything in a dense, heavy curtain of gray. Exiting the restaurant and heading out the revolving doors to the parking lot, it was as if they were entering a surrealist inversion of the outside world. All the neon signs were swaddled in mist and had become incandescent ciphers, stripped of their commercial significance by their immersion within the mist, leaving only the vari-colored beauty of their mysterious, unearthly radiance. The ever-present sounds of hundreds of slot machines became muffled as they drifted out into the cold evening air, transformed into a dim, vague ringing that reverberated dully through the parking lot like one long, sustained chord, the sound of a submerged orchestra wafting up from the murky chambers of the sea.

After savoring the memory, Celeste got out of bed and dressed for the day, then packed away the rest of her belongings into the suitcase. She took one last look at her room and headed downstairs. At nine in the morning, most of the on-site staff had already eaten their breakfast, so Celeste ate alone, staring contentedly out the oriel windows which looked out onto the front lawn. Off in some distant room, she could hear someone playing Chopin's *Raindrop Prelude* on piano, stopping at one particular point in the mid-section and repeating the part over and over with varying degrees of success.

Having arranged for a taxi to pick her up at ten, Celeste decided to go look at the forest one last time. She walked up the familiar path to the edge of the woodland and stood there at its threshold. Staring into those depths, she felt again the sensation of looking into a measureless well, and she sensed once more the quietude which reigned within that living museum of trees.

A soft wind blew by, sending rippling waves through the many leaves of the various kinds of trees represented there — pine, oak, beech, spruce. In that moment, Celeste was seized with a wild urge to discard her suitcase and obligations and simply run into the woods; the thought rose up within her with a startling violence, but quickly on its heels came the knowledge that she could not realistically do so, a knowledge that came with a stinging sadness.

Celeste became aware that she was biting her lip to keep herself from crying, though she did not really know quite why. It was not, she knew, the forest itself that she desired to see, nor the people or things she had encountered there. It was something else.

In the distance, like a familiar voice calling her back to the world, came the sound of a car pulling up. Turning, Celeste saw a beige taxicab coming down the driveway. She picked up her suitcase and walked toward it.

40.

As the taxi bore her away, Celeste stared somberly out the window at the grand estate now receding from view. Beyond the manor, like a green wall, rose the southern face of the forest, looking as lush and inscrutable as it had on the first day she arrived.

Celeste's mind turned to the future: to the great black or silver train that she would board in Berlin, and the airport it would convey her to, and beyond that, the plane, the landing, the burnt-red Datsun that her parents would pick her up from Tucson International in, and the long drive home through the Sonoran Desert to the town of Patagonia. The familiar shapes of the Patagonian Mountains would rise in the distance, those steep sky islands which to Celeste signified the landscape of home. And beyond this lay the rest of her life: jobs, friends, apartments, houses, age, maybe marriage, maybe kids.

She thought of her brother Fernão and his obsession with car culture, and the hypnotic lure of neon signs and long dark highways. There was something about a sleek, glistening machine floating over a belt of asphalt as it cut through the Arizonan wilderness, gliding past the silhouettes of jagged rocks and barrel cacti — the primal potency of the desert juxtaposed with the streamlined promise of modernity. She thought of the auto body shop Fernão now worked at, pulling long hours to support his family, and the way that some nights, when she was over visiting, he'd excuse himself after dinner and go out alone into the front yard, staring off at the horizon and listening to the wind whipping across the vast plains.

She thought of Anise living with her husband in their dwelling by the forest's edge, quietly rehearsing the rhythms of a pre-modern lifestyle while the broader world around them rushed relentlessly forward, their village a slow eddy within a fast-moving river. She thought of Holzfäller's crumbling estate, and the windows of the glass palace that lay shattered and open to the sky. She thought of the dew-sodden eaves of the Black Forest, and marble columns upon pediments beside still pools, and the evening lights of Venetian apartments glistening upon the dark waters of the canal, and the wave-lashed cliffs of Big Sur with towering redwoods lining the sandy precipices like sentinels, and the shining face of the moonlit Urubamba river as seen from the air, a serpentine line winding its way through the jungle. And she thought of a beach somewhere: cool and long, with black waters lapping upon the empty shore, the pin-prick fires of distant suns glowing high above, and sea-birds floating over the silver-tipped waves, and everything waiting, waiting, waiting.

www.ingramcontent.com/pod-product-compliance
Lightning Source LLC
Chambersburg PA
CBHW030940210726
48290CB00007B/2272